THERE GO I

A NOVEL BY

Many -
I'm very pleased and so
to know you and
happy to have had you join
the cast of the Star Trek show!
I hope you enjoy my novel!
Jay P. Michaels

Jay P. Michaels

PAGE PUBLISHING, INC.
New York, NY

Originally published by Page Publishing, Inc. 2017

ISBN 978-1-64082-265-8 (Paperback)
ISBN 978-1-64082-266-5 (Digital)

Printed in the United States of America

I telled him it. I telled him the whole thing,
upside down on a box.
　　　　　　—from the time travel journals of
　　　　　　　　　　　Dr. Henry Maris

Maris was fifty-four years old when he wrote the above passage in the spring of 1967. The "him" referred to would be born a year later, conceived of a drug-influenced union in the Summer of Love with a girl he loved some thirty years ago. A few weeks after he wrote those words, she would meet him for the first time.

His death would occur in the year 2051 at the age of eight hundred or more, alone. Not that he would be alone in the dying; the largest number of humans to ever die at one time would die with him that day, and nearly every living thing on the face of the planet Earth would die along with him.

All that would survive the comet strike would be a handful of people not living on earth and a few more who lived beneath its surface in a state of suspended animation. The humans who died the same day as Maris would have thought him to be a man in his sixties, maybe seventies, but no one saw him that day; he was, as I said, alone.

You can call me Jonah. I take my name after another man who was swallowed by a whale after refusing the call of God. I too was swallowed, but by something much bigger. This account is my arrival in Nineveh. My testimony of what I know.

I died many deaths in 2051, yet I live on. But this is not my story. It is yours. It is about how you and your world came to be. The creation and evolution of life on planet Earth, life as you know it and life as you do not know it, nor have even imagined it.

It is a story with many oranges; a story with DNA; a story with crucifixions, suicides, and resurrections, failures and victories, love, lust, rape, and murder. A story of desperation and heartache, of science and religion. The story of life. So pass the bottle or pass the blame, but here is the truth. The truth as I now know it.

***

There was no pain, as he lifted his head a quarter of an inch for the first time in three days. Dried vomit had glued his face to the carpet where he lay motionless for all this time. There was a deep humming not only in his ears but also echoing into his chest and his shoulders. He could hear the hum vibrating his skull in a strangely pleasing way, and then he dropped it back to the floor and fell back into a deathly, deep sleep.

He was somehow rolled over that instant, and his eyes were pried open by a bright sky above him, or maybe just a light—bright, blindingly bright white. Deep cave-like voices struck, echoing vibrations into his skull, and blurred colors danced a circle around his head.

His own voice took shape from somewhere outside him, outside the room where he lay looking up to the ceiling. His voice moved into him and escaped again from deep in his throat. "I should have slit my wrists," the voice said and echoed through the cramped living area he was being wheeled through, toward the door of his tiny apartment. Then he was asleep again.

***

Duncan Ryder sat up once again. The numbness he felt was familiar, and so was the returning hum and pleasurable vibration of his skull. It was reminiscent of the time he was clocked soundly with a shovel in the back of the head for planting the broccoli seeds too close together. This time, there was no sticky blood matted in his hair.

He made a slow rolling motion with his head to see the room around him. He could not seem to move his eyes independently so his entire head rolled. Two windows. One was obscured by a screen of plastic mesh, mesh that would prevent him from opening the window to jump out or from breaking it and using the shards of glass as a weapon on himself. The other window was designed to allow the nurses to see into the room from the desk and observe his every move.

Next to the bed, on a rolling table, was a stack of papers. He moved his arm in a slow arch to pick up one of the papers; delicately he grasped onto it, lifted it up in front of his face. It was his admission papers. Where his signature should be, there was a wavy line that trailed off the edge of the paper.

He had no memory of signing anything, yet there were stacks of papers showing he had been on his apartment floor for three days and here in a drugged stupor for another three.

He was unaware of the world for nearly a week. That was not long enough for his liking.

Some people think those who try to kill themselves inwardly want to be stopped, for someone to interfere with their plans. That is not true at all.

They may not have the guts to carry out a truly fatal self-inflicted injury, but salvation is not what they are seeking or longing for. The only thing they want from the outside world is a motive, a reason to stay. It is a need for life to hold some meaning for them that makes it worth living further. For some, the fear of death's secrets is motive enough; and for others, it is the promise of hope or love being renewed in their life.

Ryder had not found that reason to go on living. Not since he lost his wife and family.

He briefly found solace in the love and trust of his own family members. His brother and sister-in-law took him in when he was all alone and deeply depressed. He felt loved again.

But that changed dramatically from love and tolerance to spite and bitterness. His depression seemed like it was contagious, and he was put out on his own.

There was no such thing as love, he now told himself. He knew better; nothing in the world could make up for his loss, so bitterly cold and painful, but the love he had for his wife.

When he was still with her, he was certain no one ever loved another human the way he loved her. Now he was certain that no one ever hurt as much as he hurt from losing her.

Duncan put down the paper and looked at his empty hand; the palm of his right hand was bandaged with a gauze bandage. On the back side of the hand, a needle was securely taped into place, entering his vein for intravenous feeding or drugs or both.

"Hello, Mr. Ryder," a sickeningly perky voice suddenly chimed. "How are you feeling?" It was one of the nurses. She wore blue pants and a matching shirt, with smock-like jacket on top that had teddy bears all over it. The bears had on doctor's coats, nursing uniforms, or thermometers in their mouths, bear doctors and nurses tending to the needs of sick bear patients.

Duncan regarded her with a lazy, bitter contempt and rubbed his head wearily. "How do I feel? I feel like God was too busy spankin' his monkey to call me home."

She wore a tiny cross-shaped pin, and this was not the first time she had heard her Lord and Savior blasphemed by a patient on the ward. But this time, she had trouble hiding her offense. Maybe it was difficult to hear the term "spankin' the monkey" applied to God.

She took his wrist in her hand to check his pulse and with false pleasantry replied, "So now you're mad at God?"

He rolled his heavy head to face her, to look at her, but she was watching her wristwatch and counting the beats of his heart. His words formed, it seemed to him, from somewhere outside himself, but they were his own words so he said them anyway. "God is a great big fuck wad, ass monkey."

Now she felt he was just trying to get a rise out of her, so she would not let it get to her. She raised an emotional wall against his assault.

He was aware his words were hurtful to her, but getting a rise out of her was not his intention, just a coincidental side effect; he took no thought to the risk of her feelings. It was just that when he lost the will to live, he also lost his sense of compassion for those who found, in Jesus or in any other religious path, the reason to live that had somehow eluded him.

Besides that, he really believed that God was incompetent, a bungling creator who did not care about human pain; or maybe He was impotent, unable to do anything for anyone.

He focused his fogged mind's attention on the cross pin she wore. He allowed a flicker of guilt to enter, and then it turned to pity. Pity for her and her devotion to an uncaring and impotent God who didn't give a rat's ass about whether or not she showed any love or loyalty.

The bitterness toward the uncaring God who showed less compassion than he himself tapped Duncan on the shoulder, said. "Hey, let me express a little damned contempt." The cruelty formed from outside the four corners of his head and came together. He could watch the words leave his own lips as if they were an entity of their own, with their own agenda and purpose.

"The God you put your faith and trust in is nothing but a deadbeat dad," he said, with a sad certain air.

The nurse had taken offense at his first comment in silence. The profanity was far more at issue to her than the accusation that God did not care, that he was a "deadbeat dad." He may as well have said "red meat bad." She did not even hear him.

The words just bounced off her emotional wall and echoed back in Duncan's own ear, an ear that was already convinced the remark was true; he needed no persuasion.

The nurse was now pumping the cuff of the blood pressure device tightly around his arm, too tightly, as though she were trying to punish his nastiness with physical discomfort. It was a sort of passive aggression that Duncan knew well.

Now, he realized he felt no compassion for her, but instead a mild annoyance at the inferiority he saw in her. Much later in his life, Duncan would come to see the God in everyone.

How many emotions had he, in his hazy, drug-clouded mind, just cycled through?

Yes . . . the mood swings were back. Ryder had never known an emotion that lasted more than a few moments before his mood zipped to another emotional peak or valley. His mood swings were often so rapid that it was like a strobe light. Arbitrary too. He may have a sudden impulse to laugh out loud at the sight of a horrific tragedy or he may cry like a baby at a dog food commercial.

He remembered fondly sitting on the bed with his wife, their legs touching, he having just told her about his so-called mood disorder. She held his hand and squeezed it lovingly, saying, "We will get through this *together*."

She had assured and soothed him so convincingly that it somehow turned down the strobe light intensity of his roller coaster emotions. He found in her a stability that he never knew. A strange assurance that all was right with the world.

This translated into a strengthening of his faith. Suddenly he was believing in God again. God, he in fact believed, had given this woman to him in order that he may be complete.

As he now remembered, the moment he last saw her, wearing a black dress as though she was on her way to a funeral, he superimposed a fictional memory, one of the lid on his coffin closing and her walking away, no tears.

He had lost her forever, and that knowledge whacked him in the head now, just like the shovel had done to him some twenty years ago when he planted the broccoli too close together.

This pain, this ripping, tearing, breaking down of his soul and the disposal of his entire system of belief and the rape of his faith and trust, this is why he had taken the two bottles of Valium. This is why he wanted to die. And why didn't he die?

He thought back. He recalled the dried vomit that glued his head to the floor when the EMTs came in. He had thrown up most of the pills undigested before he lost consciousness; before he shed the mortal coil, he parted with the contents of his wrenching, twisting stomach. It was not him realizing this; it was the thought realizing him.

At that moment, he reached an epiphany. He should not have tried to overdose to begin with. He should have slit his wrists as he said a few days ago in his apartment.

"Maybe I should have taken my Valium with a little Mylanta," he mumbled, and he chuckled almost inaudibly. But it was just as well if it had been inaudible, as the nurse was the only one who could hear him and she was listening to nothing but the pulsing sound of blood going through the veins of Ryder's arm as she deflated the cuff more slowly than necessary.

Psych wards are a living hell where people are punished for not dying when they tried to. The staff are trained and practiced at helping to motivate the patients toward independent life outside the walls. The only effect on the patient is an all-consuming desire to escape. And escape is what they failed to do in the first place, the reason they are there. There is no escape. Ever.

***

The nurse now wore an American flag on her uniform where the cross pin had been before. This was a growing trend outside the four walls of the psych ward. In the real world, American spirit was surging like never before while U.S. planes dropped bombs on a country called Afghanistan.

Many of Duncan's companions on the ward could not stop obsessing about the recent attack on the World Trade Center. Unnatural fears gripped a few of them. Now, the group of them sat in the common room together, as they did three times a day, and tried to come to cope together.

Robert, an out-of-work dot-commer with a four-day-old beard and stitches on his wrists, said to the group, "I just don't see how God could let something like this happen."

Duncan stared off and absentmindedly spoke under his breath. "You ain't seen nothin' yet," he said. He was quoting the Prophet.

***

This is how the Almighty God doing business as a man named Elias Parker, a resident of Cheney Home, came to be known as "the Prophet."

Duncan Ryder was leafing through a fat notebook that sat in his lap. On every page, he left his initials in green ink inside a little box. He was only going through the motions, his attention really focused on the glowing television, which showed rescue dogs and their police masters working by artificial light to find survivors or victims amid the rubble of what was once a federal building in Oklahoma.

It was 3:00 a.m., but Tylee Christiansen and Elias Parker were both up and watching CNN with Duncan. Neither was there for the live report or because they could not sleep.

Both were strongly attracted to Duncan, though for different reasons, and they were both only there to be in his presence. They were there to somehow draw strength or wisdom or joy from being with him.

He had no idea they were there for him, and his attention was focused upon neither of his companions.

The television coverage showed the rescue site from the air to show how the lights had been arranged to light the entire structure. It struck something in Duncan that resembled awe, perhaps a cross between awe and pity. "Jesus!" he exclaimed with an emphatic and reverent whisper.

The Prophet, who was known at that time as Elias Parker or sometimes as "the Weatherman," spoke up, reminding Ryder he was not alone. "You ain't seen nothin' yet!" he said in a knowing tone that seemed eerily lucid and very real.

Elias had schizophrenia, and most of the time, the things he said did not make the little hairs on Duncan's neck stand up. But tonight, his words seemed ominous. A chill ran through him, which was interrupted by the warmth of Tylee's voice. She had ignored Elias. She wanted Duncan to notice her just then, so she spoke out as if to no one.

"How," she asked to the air or to the television, "could God allow such a thing to happen?" She knew Duncan was outspoken about his agnosticism, and she wanted to impress him with her own doubts although they were not as strong as those of Duncan, the eternal skeptic.

The face of Elias Parker lit like the searchlights on CNN and radiating with warmth, wisdom, and joy. He crossed the room and took hold of each of Tylee's hands in his. He looked her in the eyes with warmth and love and said, "Mah dear, dear child! De man who has nevah walked een de darkness takes de light for granted." He smiled first at her and then at Duncan, and then he walked into the hallway and turned toward his room.

Ryder leaned out of his chair to watch him stride down the hall, and the fat notebook fell from his lap to the floor.

He had noted Parker's unusual talent for predicting the weather and had been pointing it out to the entire nursing staff for months. He would hold the newspaper up and ask, "Elias, what's the weather going to be like tomorrow?" He would then read the forecast from the paper, and if Parker's prediction differed from the paper, it was always Parker who was right. This phenomenon earned him the nickname of Weatherman. But at that moment, Elias's talent seemed to Ryder to be wisdom, not some sort of internal barometer.

That night, Ryder changed Parker's title from Weatherman to Prophet, and it never left him ever after even though Ryder himself dismissed it as a mere nickname and misinterpreted the visions of the future the Prophet shared with him throughout the next few months of their acquaintance.

***

This is how the Almighty God believing himself to be a suicidal man living in a psych ward found his ticket out of the hospital.

Tylee Christiansen looked at her father with her skeptical head turned at a slight angle. She knew what was coming.

After twenty hours in the hospital, she was still there. In the cafeteria. The surgery was successful, but she would never get her father to relent now. He would keep needling her until she agreed to get a nurse to come check on her from time to time.

She felt visiting nurses were a sign of doom, like angels of death. She may be crippled, but she was not dying, goddamnit!

"Ty honey," he began and cleared his throat, "I know you don't want to hear this—"

"No, Daddy, I don't! I am okay without a nurse, really."

"Well, how about this . . . Why not clear all my stuff out of the den and we can rent out the room? Not necessarily to a nurse, just someone who can keep an eye on you. That way, it won't cost us anything, and we will have someone there with you during the day. I'd feel safer if you had someone there when you got home from work."

Tylee groaned and hung her head.

"Honey, just to shut me up. So I feel better."

She raised her head up again. "You will never be happy, Dad. It's not in your nature."

"I just don't want you to be alone if something should happen," he went on, ignoring her invitation to make the conversation about his idiosyncrasies instead of her need for a babysitter.

"Jesus, Dad, I wish I could be alone!" she exclaimed with a loud exhale of sincerity.

She immediately realized she was alone except for her nag of a father. Despite all his overprotectiveness, she loved him to death. And now she had wounded him, even if only a little.

She quickly turned to an apologetic mode. "I didn't mean it like that, Daddy. I love you. It is just that I work so hard to be independent, but I could never afford an apartment of my own. Without you, I would not have a place to stay. Nothing."

She was apologizing. This was how Dr. Christiansen knew he had taken her too seriously again. Now he felt compelled to lighten the mood, to smooth the path again. "An apartment?

Shoot, girl! Even I can't afford an apartment in Northern California!"

She smiled, and he knew that wicked little grin well. It was his first indication that she was back to herself again. No more apologizing for his hypersensitivity.

"You would be rollin' in dough if you just patented your work," she teased. "Just give up on your ideals of pure research and bow to the almighty dollar, Pop."

"Ty honey, instant millionaires are made by game shows and web-based startups, not by quantum physics."

"Okay, Dad, great idea. Let's run with that. We'll put your work on the web and make a mint."

"Better yet, we can put a game show on the web."

"They are already there." She laughed.

He looked at her for a moment, smiling with pride leaking out like uncaptured sunbeams. He leaned forward and kissed her forehead. This is something he often did when he looked at her and saw her mother. And this time was no exception. Actually, he made it an exception because this time, he not only saw her mother but also mentioned her out loud.

"I love you so much, Tylee. You make me laugh and you always believed in me. Not even your mother believed in me like you do."

Tylee would have given up the use of her arms as well as her legs if to do so would allow her to have her mother back.

Mrs. Christiansen had died in a car crash when Tylee was thirteen years old. For reasons her father never shared, he blamed himself for the death of his wife. He blamed himself and his last failed experiment.

One time, about three months ago, Christiansen had mentioned his wife in conversation, and they both became melancholy thinking about her. It led to an all-night father-daughter drinking binge.

But not this time. When her father leaned forward to kiss her forehead, the love of Tylee's life came into view. There was not a moment for the thought of her mother to depress her now. Not with this new discovery. It was him; it made no sense, but it was him. Three tables away. Was it possible?

"Duncan!" she called out so loud anyone would have turned if their name was Duncan, Dick, Harry, or Lucifer. "Duncan Ryder!"

***

This is how the Almighty God believing himself to be a colonel named Todd Guinness became a huge influence in world politics without ever being elected to any office. In fact, he remained quite anonymous to anyone without the highest of security clearances.

Surrounding oneself with greater minds can do a lot for one's career. It was what allowed Todd Guinness to rise to the rank of colonel. And it was what got him his cushy job in the CIA, an agency that never asked him too many questions, but allowed him to work with little to no interference.

Ultimately, his tendency to steal thoughts and ideas, and his aloof nature about his own ideas and thoughts, would allow him, although scientifically inept, to be responsible for the creation of the first time-travel technology. It is how he made it possible for the first human colony on another planet and possible for the first human contact with an alien race, and how he unknowingly created the origin of religion on planet Earth. And all he was trying to do was to find a better way to spy on foreign nations.

In a place called Vietnam, when he was a captain, Guinness was part of a team that employed supposed psychics to find the enemies hidden in jungles and caves. None of the psychics was nearly as effective as the Prophet, but they did have some success.

Long before the first orange was destroyed by the Marisian Rift, Colonel Guinness was using the rift for something called "remote viewing." For years after the war, they studied and experimented with psychics for remote viewing, with results that were spotty enough to hold their interest, but nothing they could use as any kind of applied science.

The discovery of the rift changed that equation. The psychics found Maris through the rift; they just had no idea how their strange abilities for remote viewing actually worked, relying completely on a vague perception of other places through the rift.

Maris was immediately made a part of the team, but somehow, he managed to get his son Eddie clearance to work as a custodian in the CIA on his brand-new top secret project.

"The singularity that is the rift," Dr. Maris explained to Guinness, "is about the size of a water molecule, and it whips around through time and space like a pinhole, so if we can peer through that pinhole to another location where the singularity also appears, we can see the remote events exactly how they happen or already happened."

"That's exactly what I want you to do, Doctor."

"Yes, and by the process I have discovered, I can actually attract together, at one time, the singularity in one spot. It's like I am widening the pinhole to a small window, albeit with limitations of course."

"Limitations?"

"Yes. It will be like looking through a wall with thousands of little pinholes or like a screen that obscures the image. Think of each pinhole as a pixel, but there is empty space between the pixels."

"So it's low resolution."

"Yes. It's like a ghost image—you can see through it, but the miracle is that you can see the image of a place on the other side of the earth."

"Great." Guinness smiled. "Let's get started."

***

After a week of confinement under close scrutiny, Duncan had finally been granted "hospital privileges." That meant he could leave the ward but had to stay on hospital grounds, and he had to remain under supervision of some staff member who may be willing to sign him out. So this outing to spend his food voucher on coffee and a danish seemed like a vacation. Like a summer trip to Niagara Falls.

His escort, Jim McManus, the hospital's recreation therapist, seemed like a best friend. Life on a psych ward is designed to make leaving a welcome and make it something to look forward to with enthusiasm.

McManus was a twenty-year-old kid with lots of energy. His life goal was to become a physical education teacher in a local high school. He made almost as much money doing his part-time stint at the hospital as he would as a teacher, maybe a little more than the phys ed teacher who taught Ryder as a kid. He had gone to a private school, a parochial school where the teachers were paid little more than volunteers.

Ryder looked across the table at his "parole officer." He silently mused, *There could not possibly be a perkier person on the planet.*

"So if you want out of this place, Duncan, you have to play their little game," he was saying.

"Basketball?" Ryder said wryly.

McManus laughed. "No, that is my game. And you don't suck as bad as you think you do at hoops, by the way."

"I just played well because I had a week's worth of pent-up energy."

"Seriously, Duncan, you know what they want out of you," Jim said.

"Yeah," Ryder grumbled. "They want my wallet! What is my bill up to now? Probably enough to put you through another year of college."

"I'll talk to the hospital administrator." Jim laughed. "Maybe we can start a team and get us both basketball scholarships."

Just then, a pretty blonde in a wheelchair screamed out Duncan's name from a couple of tables away. Both men turned toward her as she wheeled her way expertly around the tables and pulled up to them.

"Duncan!" she squealed with delight. "I can't believe it!"

Ryder's cry of recognition went up a whole octave from normal. "Tylee! Oh my god!" McManus now realized he had never seen Duncan really smile before.

"Yes! It's me! But what on earth are you doing out here in California? Did you get a job out here? What?"

He stood up, and in response to her outstretched arms, he gave her a giant hug as he answered, "No jobs."

"I heard you got married, had some kids, and moved to Iowa or something."

He sat back down, but only on the edge of the chair. He leaned toward her, like a cold man leaning toward a fire, as he spoke to her. "I did!" He beamed with a huge smile. "I even found Jesus!"

"You found Jesus? So where was he?"

Ryder chuckled. "In Iowa all these years, it seems. At the church down the block from our place. I think he was bonkin' my wife, though. Everyone else in the neighborhood was, it seems."

"So now you know how that feels, huh? So is that why there is no ring on your finger?"

He hung his head in mock shame and then raised it again and said, "Legally separated!" He reached out and took her hand tenderly in his. He held up her bare ring finger and looked into her eyes again with a spreading grin.

"Nope," she said. "No husbands for me. I am married to my chair."

"That chair is a cruel slave master of a husband!" Duncan declared with genuine sympathy.

"Yeah, it sucks." She gestured behind her at the tall skinny man who had silently come to stand behind her. "This is my dad, by the way. The only man in my life now."

The two men shook hands, and Ryder sat back down at an angle that showed he was not planning to introduce his companion to the visitors. McManus took the cue with great tact and subtlety and looked deeply interested in the surface of his coffee cup, where he could see his own reflection faintly staring back at him with a curiosity and genuine interest in him.

This was not smooth enough to ease off the curiosity of Dr. Christiansen, the quintessential overprotective father. Having been introduced and granted his inclusion to the reunion, he pried into the abyss of Ryder's discomfort. "So," he began, looking at Ryder's wrinkled T-shirt and sweatpants, the same clothes he had slept in and just played a half hour's worth of basketball in, "you here at the hospital for a job interview then?"

His daughter reached back and punched him in the arm as a reprimand for his rudeness.

McManus now looked up from his coffee cup and extended his hand as if nothing else had been said. "I'm Jim McManus, sir. Pleasure to meet you." He shook hands with a grip so firm it was almost aggressive. "I am the recreational therapist here at the hospital, and to be honest, we were just discussing Mr. Ryder's job prospects when you and your daughter came over."

Duncan scooted back in his chair with discomfort. Now he was looking at his face reflected on the surface of his own coffee. A sad face. A face he recently tried to fix so it would never be looking back at him or at anyone. "We were talking about a basketball scholarship." He sighed. "That hardly counts as a job prospect."

Tylee's face suddenly brightened. "Duncan," she said, "I have the perfect job prospect for you!"

Dr. Christiansen interrupted. "Honey, no. You can't be serious."

"I'm totally serious, Daddy," she said without turning her head. She was looking at Duncan, the man she never stopped loving. "We can't pay much, but the job is yours if you want it."

"Job? What job?" Ryder knew well that finding a job could be his ticket out of this hellish existence. Of course, he would have to live in a halfway house for a while. He would have to be supervised by hospital personnel and maybe come to therapy sessions once or twice a week, but that was better than once or twice a day! He would take any job she had for him.

"You can be my nurse."

"Nurse?"

"Well, not really. Just move in to the spare room, rent-free. All you have to do is be there to help me out if I have a problem. Maybe drive me to work or something. Help me cook and clean once in a while."

Duncan nearly fell out of his chair. "You're serious?" he said with joyous disbelief.

"Jesus, did I not just say I was serious?"

"You did say that," Jim said. He was pleasantly amused. He knew this was the key to help Ryder not only play "the little game," but he could now actually win. She was offering him a home and a job.

"Well, I do need a place to stay," Ryder said, "but I feel like I should pay you for a room. I don't want you to feel like you owe me something."

"But I do owe you something, Duncan. You lost your job because of me."

"That was just one job. A job that really sucked. And I don't hold you responsible for that anyway."

But Tylee held herself responsible. She *meant* to offer him the room and the job her father wanted for someone else. She *meant* to apologize and make amends for the past. She meant to say, "But I AM responsible, and I am sorry." The words that came out were truer than her intentions, but she immediately wished they had never burst forth from her lips. Her true words were these: "But I still love you!"

There followed a long painful silence. Even the tactfully skillful and ever-perky recreational therapist had nothing to say to soften the blow of the silent air. Tylee herself broke the silence with a whispered apology. "Oh my god! I'm so sorry!"

Ryder used his own embarrassment to soften the tension as though trading off embarrassment would cancel each of them out and level the playing field. "I'm here now because I took a whole lot of Valium and woke up in the psych ward," he said.

"Duncan!" Tylee cried. "Oh my god! Why would you do that?"

Ryder exhaled loudly and slowly. "Long story!" he muttered.

"Well, I got lots of time," she said.

Tylee Christiansen suddenly became her own mother. At least that is how it appeared to her father, the only observer that ever really knew them both.

He missed his wife so much even though she controlled him and even pushed him around a lot. A very passionate and very forceful woman Mrs. Christiansen had been. And he loved her for that.

"Daddy," she commanded, "have the room ready for Duncan tomorrow. Whatever he needs to be discharged, we'll do it." She turned to Ryder and leaned toward him. "You are my new companion. You will be getting free room and board and a small compensation. You will not have to do anything but help me cook and clean and drive me places. And you must promise not to take your own life as long as you are in my employ." She paused a moment and then added, "And I will not take no for an answer."

"But—"

"Nyet!" she chided. "You are hired! You start tomorrow. No more argument!"

And there was no argument.

***

As Duncan was passing the nurse's station, he thought about actually signing his own release papers, but he knew the nurse would just give him the runaround. She would say he needed the doctor's signature for his release.

Another patient was at the desk complaining to the nurse. "They could have AIDS," he said. He grabbed Duncan by the arm as he came close. The man positioned Duncan in front of the nurse for her consideration. "This guy," he said, "could have AIDS." He was gripping both of Ryder's arms, and it hurt just a little.

Duncan looked over his shoulder at the man who held him tightly. "David," he said quietly. That was the patient's name. Duncan had met him in the last group therapy session.

David had been admitted that morning. He came to the morning therapy group with a timid tremor throughout his body. He wiped the chair with a handkerchief from his back pocket and sat down slowly and carefully as though he were lowering himself into a hot bath.

"David," Duncan repeated. Still quietly, he went on even though David said nothing back. "I do have AIDS." David stared at him in silence.

"And," he lied, "I licked every single spoon in the hospital."

This part was true: "And right now, you're squeezing my arm where they gave me an IV, and you could squeeze out some blood."

David loosened his grip and released him. He checked his hands for blood as Duncan turned to face him. Ryder smiled wickedly and looked David in the eye.

David pulled out his handkerchief and began to frantically wipe his hands as he shrieked. The shriek built into a panicked scream as he turned to run to his room.

The nurse followed, trying desperately to calm him.

Ryder went to his room. All he grabbed was his toothbrush though he wasn't sure why. It was one the hospital provided for him anyway.

Gripping the toothbrush as though it were a precious gem, he calmly but quickly strode out the back door of the ward.

By the time he hit the down button on the elevators, an out-of-breath nurse was standing at his side.

"You can't leave without an escort," she panted. "Where are you headed?"

"I'm going home."

"Home? You can't go home. You need an escort just for hospital privileges. You have to have a pass to go home, just like anybody else."

"Do you have to earn a pass?"

"I'm an employee. That's different."

"You said 'like anybody else.'"

"You are still a patient at this hospital! And I'm your charge nurse. You can't go."

"But I was not committed against my will. I signed my own admission papers. Remember?"

"That's right. You signed them yourself."

"Well, I now revoke my consent to treatment. You can't keep me against my will."

"Well, the doctor can."

"Okay. You go get him. I'll wait right here."

The elevator made a ding sound, and the door opened. Duncan stepped in, smiled, and waved with one hand and pressed the ground floor button with the other.

"You said you would wait!" she shouted as the doors closed.

Soon she was back at the nurse's desk calling security. The guard was waiting at the elevator on the ground floor at the nurse's request. They would hold him just long enough for a doctor to sign an order that would allow them to hold the patient against his will.

But Duncan was not on the elevator. He had gotten off on the third floor, walked past the OR waiting area, and took the side stairs to the ground floor, where he met his waiting ride at the side of the building.

***

Dr. Christiansen patiently waited for the car door to shut before he even opened his mouth to unload his burdened mind.

"Okay," he said, as he turned the ignition key, "I am helping you because my daughter insists you are worth it. Her, I trust implicitly. You, however have yet to earn my trust."

"Daddy!" Tylee spoke up, blocking the tirade. "I told you he lost his job because of me! I owe him. And he would never hurt a flea. I trust him even if you don't."

"Ty honey, I just helped a man I don't know escape from a psych ward. Do you expect me to be okay with that?"

"Would it be easier if I told you how I lost him his job?"

Duncan said nothing, but his eyes begged Tylee to never mention it again.

"Maybe it would help," her father said, "but what I really want to know is why he was in the hospital to begin with."

"Okay," Ryder agreed. "We can stop for some coffee, and I'll fill you in on my whole story."

"We have coffee at home," Christiansen said. "I don't want to be seen with you in public just yet."

***

Duncan took a first sip of coffee and made a pained expression that Christiansen thought must mean the coffee was either too hot or plain tasted bad.

"Do you need some cream or sugar?"

"Oh no," Duncan said. "I always drink it black." He sipped again, with less of a pained expression. "Do you know the story of Job?"

"You mean from the Bible?"

"Yes. Do you know that story?"

"Yeah. I'm familiar with it."

"You know," Ryder said, "that story always made me hate God."

"Why?"

"Well, He's got this guy he supposedly loves, and the devil comes along and they make a little bet. So God rips away everything from Job. His money, his home, his family, and even his health. Job's on the street covered in boils and still refuses to curse God."

"Right," Christiansen agreed. "It's a story of great faith. When Job remains faithful, God rewards him for it."

"Yeah, but what kind of God would play a game, wagering with the devil, and destroy the life of someone who loves him?"

Christiansen shrugged his shoulders.

"Wouldn't you say that you've grown closer to Tylee since her accident?"

"Yes. Of course! After a brief stay in Kansas, she moved back here. Now we spend all our time together."

"But you never would have crippled her yourself just so you could draw closer to her. Would you?"

"What? Of course not!"

"But that's kind of what God does to Job. And just to prove a point to the devil."

"So . . . ," Christiansen pried, "you are Job, aren't you?"

"We all are," he said. "We are God's amusing little experiments. His stakes in a game with Satan. I just decided to break the cycle. I took the advice of Job's wife and friends."

"To curse God and die?"

"Yes. But the cycle was not really broken. He didn't let me die."

"What cycle were you trying to break? It sounds like you were just helping Satan win the bet."

"The cycle of blessing and curse. Blessing and curse. So now I'm blessed again. I have a home and a job, and I'm sitting next to a beautiful woman who says she loves me."

Tylee, who was just innocently sipping her coffee, blushed and rolled her eyes. "I do love you," she said. "I always did."

Duncan snorted. "Sorry, my dear. I've just heard that line so much I can't help but be cynical."

"From me?" she asked, wounded.

"No, no. Not you. Just from every woman along the way who was part of the blessing cycle. Then comes the curse when they decide they never loved you. Instead they loved your car, or your money, or your penis, or your playing father to their kids."

Christiansen crossed his arms and slunk back in his chair, the pose of a skeptic. "Duncan, you wouldn't happen to be bipolar, would you?"

Tylee laughed. "Daddy! You switched from physics to psychiatry?"

"Actually," Duncan said, "That's what my shrink says. But it's not in my head. Oh no! Were it in my head, then the medicine would fix me."

"So what exactly does that mean? That it's not in your head? If not in your head, where is it?"

"The whole world is bipolar. God is manic-depressive. Not me."

"They say," Christiansen offered wickedly, "God only gives you what he knows you can handle."

"Right," Ryder agreed. "He tests the very limits of your endurance and then gives you little rewards. Then He tries you by fire again. That is God's bipolar cycle."

"I see." Christiansen uncrossed his legs and recrossed them the other way. "So now that I am the appointed psychologist, tell me, Duncan, about your last trial by fire. The one that ended with you taking all that Valium and winding up in the hospital."

"Okay. That would be the wife."

***

Tylee watched as Duncan carefully pulled apart his Oreo. She was taken back about ten years to when they were together at Cheney Home, where she first fell in love with him. He would pull apart his Oreos one at a time and dunk the half without frosting in his coffee and set aside the other. Then he would put two halves together, frosting side in, and pop the whole cookie with double frosting in his mouth and sip his coffee, to wash it down she supposed.

Once, she had bought a bag of the kind with double the frosting. He took the Double Stuf Oreos apart in exactly the same way and ate quadruple-stuff Oreos. "You don't have to take these apart," she said. "They already have double the frosting."

Through a mouth way too full of cookie, he said, "But where is the fun in that?"

Now with a mouth, again, way too full of cookie, he said, "I found a new reason to live."

"Why is that?" Tylee asked.

"For Oreos!" he stated. "They aren't as sweet as my wife, but they will never lie to me."

"She was sweet to you?"

"Yeah. Of course!"

"So why did you leave her?"

"Um . . . ," Duncan paused. "The cops, I think. Yeah, it was the cops who came and said I had to grab all my clothes and leave."

"The cops? Oh my god! What did you do to her?"

"Not a thing! Did I ever do anything to hurt you?"

"You hurt me more than you will ever know."

"Well, yeah, but not so cops were involved, right?" Duncan stammered.

"No, of course not!"

"So she had left me already and the cops come by the house with papers, and they say I must be removed from the premises."

"What kind of papers?"

"She had said to a judge that I posed a threat to her, so they granted her a restraining order."

"But you said she left you."

"Yeah. She just wanted me out so she could come get all the furniture and stuff. So she did not say that she was not living there. So the cops make me load up the minivan while they watched."

Tylee laughed. "You had a minivan?"

"I had a minivan."

"So where were the kids at that time?" Tylee asked.

"The kids. Ah yes. They were already gone. Wards of the state, I believe. That is part of why my wife left, I think."

"Did you hurt the kids?"

"Of course not!"

"But she thought you did?"

"Honestly," Ryder paused a long while. "I thought she hurt them. Now I don't even know anymore."

"Why did they take the kids?"

"Um, maybe I should start this story much sooner." Duncan sighed.

"How about where we left off?"

"You mean right where we left off?"

***

This is how the Almighty God doing business as a young orderly named Duncan Ryder came to be unemployed and separated from the first love of his life. And this is also where Duncan and Tylee left off.

"Duncan, I love you," Tylee said. "Somehow I think I want this more than you do."

"What? No," Duncan replied. "I'm just scared."

"Of what?"

"Of what happens if we get caught."

"You're not on the clock," Tylee said. She really believed that somehow that mattered and somehow he would be immune to any kind of retribution should someone enter the old chapel and find his penis hardening in her hand.

They were in the old chapel because it was never used. It was adjacent to the nursing home but was left untouched while the rest of the old building was razed. Even though the new facility was owned by the county, and even though a new chapel was in the new facility, there was tremendous public pressure, mostly from family members of residents, to keep the old chapel intact. It was sometimes still used for small weddings and funerals.

Duncan knew well that should anyone find him and Tylee here in this precarious circumstance, it would mean another kind of funeral—a funeral for his job at the county facility.

Not as though that would be such a bad thing anyway. He was already being considered for another job downtown at the civic center. A job that was more physically demanding, but not so stressful, a job not requiring him to squelch his scruples in exchange for assembly-line efficiency.

That was the problem with his job now. People were treated like cattle being herded from their beds to the dining room for breakfast and then to their beds again when their morning meds kicked in and made them too tired to stay awake for the day. At least in working the night shift, he could avoid most of the herding except for the last hour before the morning shift came in.

This chapel was the only place they could think of for a clandestine rendezvous of this sort, but it still made Ryder sort of uneasy, agnostic or not, to be committing a sexual act in a chapel pew. This discomfort gradually eased as Tylee lowered her lips around his shaft.

A friend of his used to say, "A hard dick has no conscience." And that could not be any truer at this moment as Tylee rubbed her spit with her hand up and down on his shaft, freeing her mouth long enough to speak.

"Tell me you love me," she said and filled her mouth again before he could answer.

"Oh, oh, oooooh!" he said, squirming on the pew. He looked up at the Protestant cross hanging on the wall behind the chancel and haltingly replied on her command, "I . . . I . . . love . . . you. Oh god! I love you!"

The Prophet, Elias Parker, met him in the parking lot the next evening just before Ryder's shift was to begin.

The Prophet smiled at him and greeted him with this advice: "If you are going to be kicked out of the garden, you may as well taste the fruit before you go."

Duncan and Tylee never found out which nurse had seen them in the old chapel, but he was called into the office as soon as he reported for his shift, the Prophet in tow. He was told to leave and never enter the premises of Cheney Home again. As an "at will" employee, and not in the union, Ryder was dismissed without a cause given, but it was clear someone had seen the two of them together.

Earlier that day, Tylee was also asked to find another facility to finish her rehabilitation.

***

This is how the Almighty God, believing himself to be a physicist named Henry Maris, described the rift that bears his name to a man called the president.

"What it actually is seems to be a singularity about the size of a water molecule," the physicist said to his tiny audience. "But the size is just our best guess because it whips around through space and time."

"A singularity is like a black hole," said his companion, Colonel Guinness.

"Doesn't a black hole suck in everything around it?" the president asked.

"Yes. But my theory is that it only attracts what we call dark matter," Maris explained.

"And that's the stuff we can't see, but we believe it exists anyway?"

"Right. And if Maris is correct, we may also be able to detect and measure dark matter with the rift," Guinness offered.

"And dark matter makes up about 84.5 percent of the universe according to estimates," Maris said.

"Did you ever notice that when a propeller spins, you can see through it?" he continued.

"Sure."

"Well, we think we can look through this thing the same way to other places and times," Guinness said. "It's possible to see and hear right into the Kremlin, Mr. President."

He knew that would get the man's attention and really pique his interest.

Maris went on. "And although you can see through a propeller, if you tried to pass through it, you would be hacked to pieces."

He pulled out his little demonstration device. It looked like a pair of wheels put together way too close. There was a small hole at the top of the front wheel, and Maris turned the device on. He could then see through the hole as the rear wheel spun around, and its holes lined up with the tiny hole in the device's front wheel.

He picked out a jelly bean from the dish on the man's desk.

"How can we safely pass this jelly bean through the hole?" he asked.

"Not that one," the president said. "I like the red ones." He handed Maris a green jelly bean. "Watermelon," he said.

"Green?"

"Put it through." He smiled.

Maris did and the bean was severed by the spinning wheel, and the back end fell to the table. Reagan picked it up and handed it to Maris.

"Just like a watermelon." He smiled. "Green on the outside, red on the inside. Taste it," he insisted.

Maris looked at it for a second. "Are there seeds I need to spit out?"

Reagan laughed, and Maris popped the bean in his mouth. It surprised him how much it tasted like real watermelon.

He grabbed an orange bean and cut it in half with the device. (Maris always had loved oranges). He picked up the severed end and examined it, like a jeweler examining an orange diamond. "No segments," he observed.

He popped the orange half a bean into his mouth and chewed, showing his approval on his face and nodding his head for a further demonstration of how much it pleased him.

"They helped me quit smoking," Reagan said. "But now I can't stop eating these damned things."

"Mr. President," Guinness butted in, "we wanted you to see this." He flipped a switch on the contraption's base. The rear wheel slowed down, and he stopped its spinning with his hand. Then he aligned the holes on the two wheels. He picked out a red bean and tossed it through the aligned holes.

The president picked it up from the table and popped it into his mouth. "If we can line up the holes, we can pass it through and still be able to eat the whole bean."

"Exactly!" said the two presenters in harmony.

"You will get your money," the president said. "I will see to it."

***

"I knew," Ryder said, pulling apart another Oreo cookie, "Cheney Home would never give me a positive job reference, and I couldn't apply for any other county job. That left the civic center job out, but as a state-registered certified nursing assistant, finding another job would be pretty easy. Then again, I did not want to work in geriatrics anymore anyway.

"So I left geriatrics, but not health care. I went to work as a caregiver for developmentally disabled clients."

"What does that mean? Developmentally disabled?"

"Mentally disabled, basically. I had lots of autistic clients and someone with Down syndrome, Asperger's, things like that."

"Oh, I see."

"I worked for a small church-supported organization where they liked me so much I was working extra hours." He smiled. "Yeah," he went on, "I worked for a church organization. My boss was actually a bishop."

"How long did that last?"

"About six months. I once worked through a snowstorm and a power outage for what turned into a thirty-six-hour shift."

"Wow. Did you get to sleep?"

"When the client was in bed, I got to sleep in the living room recliner, but I had wicked-bad insomnia, so I only got about two hours of sleep.

"Because of the snowstorm, well, blizzard, no one else could get through on the roads to relieve me from my shift, so I had to stay in a house with no power all night and all day. My only company was an autistic blind man who was completely nonverbal."

"So you couldn't even carry on a conversation?"

"Nope," he continued. "We had a battery-powered AM radio, which I played music on. That was my only real link to the world outside for those thirty-six hours."

"Must have driven you crazy."

"For sure! But my dedication seemed to impress the bishop, and he gave me a promotion, and I became what they called a 'job coach' where I helped a client do landscaping at the cemetery in the spring."

"Landscaping?"

"Well, yeah. That's what the client's job was, and my job was to be with him and make sure he followed his boss's instructions and did not talk back or yell at him or anything that would be instinctual for you or me. Fortunately, they didn't know how I lost my job as a CNA. Maybe I could have used a job coach back then myself.

"I tried to give my landscaping client plenty of room, but the other groundskeepers automatically did not like that he had me around. They refused to sit with him on a lunch break, so I sat with him while he ate . . . Not at any table, mind you, just in the rows between the tombstones."

"Kind of creepy."

"That's not the half of it!" Ryder said. "While he was eating, I looked down at the stone where I was sitting, and the name on the gravestone was Duncan Ryder."

"Your name? Same spelling even?"

"Yes. I felt like Ebenezer Scrooge."

"That IS creepy!"

"And with my insomnia, I had not slept a night in four straight days. I thought I was still having trouble transitioning off of the night shift.

"Anyway, I was still reeling from losing my other job so suddenly."

"Even after six months, you couldn't sleep at night?"

"Even after all that time," he affirmed. "But it was not from the night-shift transitions. It was my bipolar disorder causing the insomnia. And when I did sleep, I had nightmares."

"Oh, I'm so sorry."

"So I was seeing a therapist through my health insurance . . . That's the one good thing about health industry jobs: the health insurance benefits.

"And the therapist sent me to see a psychiatrist so I could get on some antidepressants. I had just started on Prozac and Valium. The Valium helped me sleep, but I had more bad dreams on the Prozac . . .

"Anyway," he continued, "I kind of went off the deep end. My new doctors say it was because I was on Prozac, and I should have been on lithium."

"Lithium? That's for manic depression, right?"

"Exactly. But it's generally referred to as bipolar disorder instead."

"Oh, I don't think I ever knew those were the same thing."

"So I'm at the hospital, and the doc tells me I need my meds adjusted. But I missed work the next day and called in. I should not have told them I was at the hospital and that I was having my medications adjusted.

"When I came out of the hospital two days later, finally having slept, I had to go talk to the bishop, and I was fired again."

"For what?"

"Well, I can't prove it, but I think it was because they found out I was hospitalized, and that's illegal. I took that as a sign from God to just get out of health care altogether."

"What about your wife and kids? I still have not heard you mention them yet."

"I met my wife at my next job."

"And what was that job?"

"Deliveryman."

"Pizza?"

"Not this time. I did that before I became a CNA though. And before my freshman year in college, I delivered water beds. But this time, I was delivering coupon books."

"Coupons?"

"Yes. There were telemarketers in a whole different state calling into our town selling coupon books. I was delivering the books and collecting the money for the telemarketers."

"Oh, that sounds like fun. Not." She laughed.

"Actually, it was kind of fun. See, there was this one telemarketer. Pretty girls started asking me about him by name after they bought the coupons from his sales calls.

"Finally, I asked to speak with this guy because I wanted to know his secret for finding and piquing the interest of pretty women over the phone. He comes on the phone with a deep, sexy baritone voice. He sounded just like Barry White."

"So he charmed your wife before you got there with her coupon book, and then YOUR charm took over?"

"Basically, that's exactly how we met. She offered me a Pepsi, and I called in for my next delivery, and they said the telemarketers were on lunch break and there were no deliveries for at least a half an hour, so I sat and had a Pepsi."

"And that was all it took, huh?" she asked slyly.

"Well, that's how it started. I asked if I could keep her phone number and she said 'Please do.' So I called her later and asked her out on the weekend, and we went out and used one of the coupons she had bought.

"It was a free go-cart rental. So we went and raced go-carts and then we played minigolf."

"Sounds like fun."

"Then after our second date, she asked me to take care of her cats while she went out of town for the Fourth of July, which I did. I spent my holiday trying to coax a cat out of a gutter where he went to hide from all the fireworks around him."

"Aw, poor kitty."

"Yes, but if I was going to impress this girl, I had to keep the poor kitty safe, so there I was lying on my stomach trying to coax the cat out of the gutter. Or at least close enough to grab him, which he finally did."

"Aw. A happy ending. That's good."

"And once he was safe, I cleaned the apartment and bought greeting cards and left them out around the place for her to find."

"Mushy, but charming. So that worked?"

"Two days later, we first got it on. So yeah, I think it worked."

"You devil." Tylee laughed.

"Two weeks later, we were engaged."

"Jesus! Two freaking weeks?"

"Two weeks." Duncan laughed.

"I moved in to her place, and we got married soon thereafter."

"No long engagement?"

"Well, I tried to. We planned a ceremony for the following year, but her pastor insisted we have a small ceremony first since we were already living together.

"He did not want his congregation to see him marry us after we had been living in sin, so to speak, so he convinced us to have a ceremony with his congregation as witnesses and have the bigger wedding later when we planned it for the following year."

"So you got married to please her pastor."

"Yeah, but at least it wasn't a bishop." He laughed.

"Anyway," he went on, "the coupon-book gig did not last long, and now I had a family to support, so I went back into health care again."

"As a nurse's aide again?"

"We moved to a small town in Iowa where I worked at a hospital in another town about ten miles away.

"After a while living there, my wife told me the older daughter was sneaking into her sister's room at night."

He paused for a long while. He put together two halves of Oreos he had already pulled apart.

Tylee spoke up. "Sneaking into her sister's room?"

"And," he continued at last, "experimenting on her sister . . . Sexually."

"Oh my god! How old were they?"

"Twelve and five."

"Five? And she was, what? Molesting the five-year-old."

Duncan nodded and wiped away a tear before he went on. "I had not been a dad for very long, and I had never dealt with anything in my life like this before."

"Hopefully, very few parents have to go through such a thing."

"Tell me about it!"

"What did you do then?"

"I called up Child Protective Services. I told them what was happening, according to my wife anyway—I never caught her in her sister's room. I was finally sleeping at night. And so I asked the CPS what to do.

"CPS had a theory that the twelve-year-old was acting out because she herself had been molested. And of course, who would they suspect more than the new stepfather?"

"Oh no!"

"I came home from work a day or two later and was told the twelve-year-old was taken out of school by the CPS agents. She was in protective custody now.

"This did not make sense to me. If they thought someone in the home . . . If they thought I was molesting her, why leave the five-year-old in the home with me?

"I called the CPS representative and said once she found out I was innocent, they could bring home the girl they had taken, but until then, I suggested they should take the five-year-old too. After all, she was the one whom we KNEW had been molested by her older sister."

"Did they come take her?"

"Yes. But then my in-laws told my wife I had called CPS in the first place in order to get them to take away the kids because I did not love them and wanted them out of the way."

"No!"

"My wife never trusted me, it seems. And she always wanted me to trust her. She'd say, 'I'm your wife. You're supposed to trust me.' I don't know why she felt I didn't trust her in the first place."

Tylee leaned forward and put her hand tenderly on his knee. "Only the untrustworthy will demand your trust. Those who deserve it know that trust is worthless if it's solicited."

Duncan considered this silently.

"Those who deserve trust," Tylee continued, "will strive to earn it with honesty and faithfulness. And then you will give them your trust freely by your own choice. They don't demand that you trust them. They prove your trust with their own worth."

Duncan paused then went on with his story. "Anyway, the older girl told the CPS agent that both my wife and I had been having sex with her, but her understanding of what that actually meant was very limited. What I was actually accused of was teaching her how to French-kiss.

"So I went to answer questions for the police, and they read my rights to me and said if they didn't like what I had to say, I would be arrested and charged."

"Oh no!"

"The police questioning was how I learned what I was actually suspected of doing. But I answered all their questions honestly, and the police were totally on my side. They said they could tell I was telling the truth, and they would not bring any charges."

"That's a relief."

"Yeah, but CPS was still involved. They told us both, my wife and me, that SOMEONE had molested the twelve-year-old at some time in the past.

"Apparently, they told my wife I was guilty. But my wife explained that as a new inexperienced father, I was never alone with the girls. I had no opportunity to do anything wrong. So then they told her I was sneaking out of bed in the night to molest her."

"Did she believe that theory?"

"Well, at that time, we knew I was bipolar, but I was NOT on meds. I had been depressed instead of manic, so I was the one sleeping through the night. And that's how my wife, getting out of bed in the dead of night, first discovered the older daughter was in the younger girl's room."

"So she knew you were innocent."

"Yes."

"Did CPS still suspect you?"

"They said not, but instead offered me another theory. They said my wife was having an affair on me with someone else who was molesting the girls while I was working at the hospital."

"Hospital? I thought you were delivering coupons."

"Oh yeah, when we got married, I went back into health care to pay the bills of the head of a household. I thought I said that."

"So you worked at a hospital."

"Yes."

"And your wife was letting someone molest her own kids? That's terrible!"

"Deplorable, but it probably was another lie. You see, I think they were trying to turn my wife and me against each other so we would turn each other in, so to speak. They lied to her and then lied to me.

"And I guess it worked on my in-laws. They told my wife she could get back the girls if she told them it was all me and then got a divorce."

"And she did?"

"Well sort of. She got a restraining order while she was staying at her parent's house, which meant that police came to remove me from the house.

"They would not let me take anything nonessential, not even pillows off the bed.

"I was so depressed I loaded up the minivan with all they would let me take and drove to California using what was meant to be the next month's car payment for gas money.

"I got here and found the rent was WAY higher than in Iowa or Kansas."

"I sure as hell found that out too." She laughed. "That's why I moved in with my father."

"So I moved in with my brother and his wife, but I was depressed and slept all night and most of the day. And his wife was not very understanding, and she got impatient with me and insisted I leave. I maxed out my only credit card to rent a cramped little efficiency place."

"Like a studio apartment?"

"Smaller even. It was a room basically. I had to share a bathroom down a hallway. There were three tenants for one bathroom."

"And I thought I had it bad at Cheney Home. I only had one roommate to share a bathroom with," Tylee said with sympathy.

"With no job prospects here, I thought I would soon be living out of the minivan, but that would be repossessed soon as well because I could not afford the monthly payments. The next month's rent was almost due, and I was going to be late on the credit card bills. I felt I had no choice. I dug out my old Valium and tried to kill myself.

"If the Valium was still full potency and had I not vomited it up, I would probably be dead now."

"Well, I'm happy you did not succeed."

Duncan put a homemade Double Stuf Oreo in his mouth and muttered, "Thank you," before taking a sip of coffee to wash down the cookie.

"Seems like you came all the way to California just to kill yourself."

"At first I was with my brother and his wife, but even then I knew that wouldn't last. I thought I might soon be homeless in November or December. I wanted to be in a warm climate when I was living out of my minivan.

"But that was repossessed while I was in the hospital where you found me the other day. They cleaned out my apartment too. Well, the landlady did. She never even gave me an eviction notice. I guess almost dying on the carpet was a violation of my lease agreement."

"Thank God you were not living in the van when it was taken."

"I will thank you and your father, but not God."

"That's right. You are agnostic, aren't you?"

"Atheist now, I think."

Duncan did not know it then, but he would not always be an atheist. He would meet God, face-to-face, but he would never bow down, never worship him. Or maybe, just maybe, one day he would.

***

This is how the Almighty God, in the form of a young college student named Tylee, came to the place where she met the love of her life, how she lost the use of her legs.

It had been a long day. Too long. Linda was driving Tylee's green Volkswagen bug (which Tylee had named Yoda) back to the college campus.

Linda, who had ridden the Orient Express two times more than Tylee (nine times in all), looked over at Tylee who slept peacefully in the seat next to her. Her gentle snoring was drowned out by the sound of the road.

Linda poked Tylee awake. "Yoda's thirsty," she said. "You wanna drive?"

"No." The rider yawned. "But I will if you need me to."

"I think I need you to," she said, as she pulled into the truck stop, just east of Topeka.

Linda stretched her leg over Yoda's hood when she came out from the bathroom. "Did you pay?"

"Yeah. Hey! Don't scratch the finish!"

Tylee placed a can of Pepsi on the roof of the car. "You know," she said, "you'd think we would enjoy sitting after all the standing in line we did today."

"No shit. But it was worth it."

"Yeah it was. I haven't even pictured what's-his-name's face all day." Tylee giggled.

"What's his name" was Dave. David Cameron, jerk first class. They'd only dated three or four months before he decided to be a player. He tried to seduce Linda last weekend.

What kind of sleazy guy would try to make it with his girl's roommate and best friend after four months? David Cameron tried, that low-life ponytail-wearing son of a bitch!

So this was a girls' weekend out. They shared a Kansas City motel room the night before. Neither slept well. Then they got into Worlds of Fun the next morning, just ten minutes after it opened.

Before lunch, they had been on the Detonator four times. In 1996, it was the first ride of its kind in the United States. On the first time it shot them into the air, Tylee's sunglasses kept going up when the ride came to a stop.

When her shades smashed to the ground, Dave didn't even know yet that he had been dumped. Not that he would have noticed. He was probably busy trying to get lucky with one of Tylee's other friends back home.

In fact, he did call her phone late that night. Neither of the two girls would ever hear his message, but it was this: "Hey, baby! It's your man. It's the weekend, so I called. Talk to you later." It was just enough to prove he had tried to reach her.

Then he hit the bars and the dance clubs. But that was no concern to Tylee anymore. She had not thought about him all day except for once when she imagined him on the Detonator flying out of his seat at the top like her shades had done.

Now, her hostility had dissolved and she knew Linda was excited to hit the bars with her again now that she was single once more. And Tylee also looked forward to that, but she and Linda would never get that chance again.

"I don't want to walk on my sore feet anymore," Tylee said. "But my legs can sure stand to stretch out." She extended her leg like Linda had done, but she raised her foot to Yoda's roof, not merely the hood.

She let out a moan, and Linda switched to her other leg. "Feels good, doesn't it?" She smiled.

"Oh yes!" Tylee sighed happily. "There is not much room in those seats to stretch out."

"But I will manage to sleep in the passenger seat."

"No. You need to keep me awake."

"Hey, ladies!" a voice called out. "You really want to stretch out? I got something that can stretch you out real good!"

It was the backseat passenger in a red Monte Carlo. The driver, who was fueling the car, reached in the open window and punched him in the arm.

The front-seat passenger called his friend an asshole. "Sorry about that," he called out. "He's drunk."

"And he'll be walking home if he's not careful!" the driver snorted.

"Let's go, Linda," Tylee said in a hushed voice so the boys would not hear Linda's name. Linda snatched the Pepsi from the roof and climbed into the car.

"You should have gotten me something without caffeine," she bitched as the headlights switched on. "How am I going to sleep?"

"I told you, you're not going to sleep. You're gonna talk to me and keep me awake."

"But you slept for the last forty miles!" Linda protested.

"Did not! My contacts are in, I can't sleep."

"Well, you were snoring, girlfriend."

"Really? Well, no wonder my eyes are burning."

"Plus you lost your shades this morning."

"Yeah. That too."

"You're okay to drive, though, right?"

"Yeah, sure," she incorrectly asserted.

If she could have known she would never walk again, Tylee would have stretched longer, even with the childish boys leering at her ass. But of course, she did not know this.

Linda was awake just long enough to take a couple of sips of Pepsi and help get them back on Interstate 70 in the right direction. But soon enough, she was sound asleep.

Tylee tuned in the radio to an AM station out of Topeka. They were broadcasting some inane talk show with a loudmouth host who criticized the media and seemed to revere former president Reagan as a god.

Tylee got angry with right-wingers, especially this blowhard.

She always felt that all politicians were dirty in some way. She believed most Republicans were power-mad, greedy warmongers. But she also felt Democrats were idealistic or elitist. Most of them, she felt, were crooked drunkards and sleazy whoremongers. The fact that Dave Cameron was a loyal Democrat only reinforced her opinions.

But, she reasoned, if she was arguing with the blowhard on the radio, she would at least not fall asleep at the wheel.

Besides, she could not get any other stations in that were not sports, religious programming, or static-ridden music. If she chose one of those, she would fall asleep for sure. Especially the sports stations from out of Omaha, Nebraska! With them, it was always about the Huskers or the College World Series. Who would want to hear a baseball play-by-play, anyway?

Tylee yawned and told the commentator he was an idiot.

Her eyes were really burning. She pinched herself at the bridge of her nose. Putting pressure there could sometimes activate her tear ducts. She thought that would help to moisturize the stinging contacts. It only helped a little.

Headlights glared in her rearview mirror. She blinked hard and slow, closing her eyes for a second at a time. Again. Now her eyes began to water.

She slowed down, hoping the car behind her would grow impatient and pass her.

Just then, the road veered left and the headlights moved from the rearview to the driver's side mirror. Tylee raised her left elbow awkwardly to block out the reflected light that was aggravating her already-weary eyes.

With her right hand, she reached up to wipe the trail of tears from her cheek. Suddenly she realized she was weaving out of her lane, and she pulled back on the wheel in a jerking motion. The car jolted, and Linda sat up in the seat.

"What's going on?" she said, wiping her eyes.

"Sorry," Tylee said sharply.

"Hey, you're not falling asleep, are you?"

"No, no . . ."

The car behind them honked and pulled suddenly around and up beside Yoda.

"Well, they just about ran me off the road, and now they're finally going to pass."

She glanced left and saw it was the red Monte Carlo from the truck stop. The passenger in the front seat was asleep with his head pressing a pillow against his window.

The driver leaned forward and waved his finger at Tylee. He was yelling and snarling something.

"What's he saying?" Linda asked.

"Hell if I know. But it doesn't look like he's saying he's sorry."

The drunk in the backseat knocked on his window and waved at Tylee. He grinned and wagged his tongue at her lewdly.

Then he stood up, crooked and awkwardly. He was unzipping his pants. He tried to wave his penis at Tylee, but she was too busy watching her lane to see him.

She was still blinking second-long blinks and praying the boys would hurry up and pass her. They did.

The drunk was still standing and trying to wag his penis as the Monte Carlo moved back to the right lane in front of Yoda.

"What is he doing?" Linda asked.

"I don't know. It looks like he's trying to find his dick," she correctly guessed. She blinked again.

"Probably so small he needs a little help." Linda laughed. Tylee laughed too, and tears came from her burning eyes.

The driver of the Monte Carlo agreed his passenger needed help. But not help to get his dick out; rather, the driver attempted to help his passenger sit down. He reached back and grabbed the rider's back pocket. He pulled on the jeans.

"Todd, sit the fuck down!" he barked.

Todd was unable to comply.

Over the hill, the Monte Carlo had rapidly overtaken a slow-moving camper. The driver reacted quickly and skillfully. His foot left the accelerator and tapped the brake firmly.

At the same time, he tried to bring his right hand back to the steering wheel. His hand was stuck in Todd's pocket, and the Levi's proved as strong as their reputation.

The standing passenger toppled over the front seat, forcing the driver into the door. The Monte Carlo skidded sideways almost instantly and rolled onto its side.

Yoda would slam into the Monte Carlo's underside in a moment that seemed to Tylee to be the same second that the brake lights first came on. And the same second her friend had just made her laugh.

She yanked the wheel to the left, hoping to swerve around the accident rather than become a part of it.

Yoda obediently zipped to the left lane, but his steering would not let her correct to the right, and it did not stay in the left lane.

Yoda's tires left the road they would never touch again, and the car threw Tylee's unbuckled roommate through the windshield. Yoda's steering wheel jammed into Tylee's body, and the impact broke her back, dooming her to never stand again, at least not in this life.

***

When the Almighty God, operating through a young man named Duncan Ryder, left his body and transitioned to an immortal, he would take many, many innocent lives. But this is how he, for the first time in his life, consciously determined the fate of another human life.

On the day after a huge late-January snowstorm, Ryder left for work early, anticipating the bad roads. The plows had done their jobs well, however, so Ryder reported to work at Cheney Home about ten minutes early. Just enough time to smoke a cigarette, but he had quit as a New Year's resolution this year, so he punched in at the clock and headed to the nurse's station on the second floor.

"Oh good," the charge nurse greeted him, "you're early. Westman is dying. He may even be dead by the time you get to his room. I want you to clean him up first thing you do."

Ed Westman had recently been transferred from the so-called Alzheimer's wing. He never stated he was on a hunger strike of any sort. He just stopped feeding himself. He stopped walking to the dining room at mealtimes. He stopped walking altogether.

The Cheney Home solution was to transfer him to the skilled nursing wing and to puree his food and force-feed him with a syringe.

Another resident who had been there before Ryder even arrived at Cheney Home had apparently long ago gone on his own hunger strike. The solution for him was to put a feeding tube into his nose and down his throat.

He lay in bed twenty-four hours a day with the feeding tube slowly pumping liquid food into his stomach. At first, Duncan had been told, his hands were tied to the bed rails so he could not pull out the feeding tube. Years of nonuse, however, calcified the man's joints, and he couldn't reach the tube if he wanted. He was frozen in a semifetal position.

Every two hours, the nursing assistants turned "Cobie" from one side to the other to prevent bedsores. His name was actually Mr. Jacoby, but they called him "Cobie."

Like Westman, Cobie was completely nonverbal. But every time he was turned from one side to the other, he would groan painfully.

Westman's force-feeding was not as extreme yet, but he was just a doctor's order away from having his very own nasal feeding tube. But not anymore, apparently. Now he was on death's doorstep.

Before the coroner would be called, a dead resident of Cheney Home had to be cleaned. Presumably, the coroners would only pick up a dead body that had been freshly cleaned. Maybe they couldn't be bothered by a smelly corpse.

Anyway, this would not be Ryder's first time cleaning a body for the coroner, but it was the first time he'd ever been ordered to clean a living person for the coroner.

Ryder found the job morbid and creepy to begin with, but Westman, although clearly about to die, was not dead yet. The blueness of his lips was spreading to his cheeks. He would surely be dead soon.

Normally, someone turning blue, struggling to breathe, would be hooked up to an oxygen tube, and his family would be called in to come visit.

This poor soul had no family, though. No Westmans came to sit with him, and the nurses did not bother to give him oxygen either. They were just waiting—waiting for him to die.

Westman had bedsores on his hips and buttocks, and his chin and neck had rotting food smeared on them. *Why didn't someone wipe his face off after they fed him from a syringe?* Ryder thought. He could see rotten food on the roof of the man's gaping mouth as well.

Ryder began to swab the toothless mouth of the dying man, who was barely breathing. Dried food came out on the swab, food that had been forced into the man's mouth through a syringe. Every swipe of Westman's mouth produced more dried food. Duncan went through about twenty disposable tooth swabs.

Deeper and deeper into the mouth Ryder swabbed until he went too far. The man gagged, and Ryder pulled the swab out. There was moldy food and a little bit of blood on the swab. The food was both hard and gooey. He'd only been fed liquid food for a week now, but this was dried out from his refusing to swallow and from his mouth breathing.

Suddenly, the man's breath came in a deep, loud, rushing gasp. He had been choking on the food he had refused to swallow. Now breathing heavily, Westman looked angrily into Ryder's eyes. His blue ashen color began to redden again to a healthy pinkish tone.

Now the man was moaning in pain. Blood, liquefied food, saliva, and mucous began to ooze out of his mouth and onto his already-dirty chin and cheeks.

By dislodging the dried food the man was choking on, Ryder had just saved the life of a man who was not quite dead. And now Westman hated him for it.

Ryder thought of "Cobie." Now, he correctly imagined, the doctor would order a nasal feeding tube for Westman.

His hands would be tied to the bed rails to prevent him from pulling out the feeding tube.

As long as Westman lived, he would spend his life in bed, being turned from side to side every two hours to prevent bedsores. He would groan in pain as he was turned, just like "Cobie."

More than one resident of Cheney Home had said to Ryder over his two years on the job, "Why don't you just kill me and get it over with?" Those were the residents privileged enough to still be able to speak. They could still visit with their families and could play bingo and listen to music and watch television.

Westman had been about to die on his own terms. And Duncan had snatched death away from him. Duncan could see the hatred in the man's eyes.

He knew he'd just been saved. But saved for a life of being fed through a tube, lying in bed with his hands tied, and being turned every two hours. They would start to call him "Westie." He would be dehumanized.

His eyes seemed to be asking Duncan why.

It occurred to the young orderly that the nurses already thought Westman was dead. No one wanted to come check on him while he was cleaning the corpse for the coroner.

He could use the pillow to finish the job the dried food had started. He could smother Westman to death and save him from being confined to a bed for years with a feeding tube up his nose.

The bed on the other side of the room was empty. They so expected him to die they put him in a room without a roommate. No one would even question the young orderly.

"You were right," he would tell the charge nurse. "He was already dead when I got there."

Ryder reached out and grabbed the nearby pillow. Somehow, though, it seemed to weigh as much as a load of bricks. He could barely lift the thing. With a great, slow effort, he raised the pillow up over Westman's head.

Westman looked up at the pillow then looked Duncan right in the eye. He breathed out and held his breath. He closed his eyes and scrunched up his nose.

Westman knew what was coming and wanted to help. He had, after all, been trying to die for the past week. He was ready now.

Ryder's head throbbed. The pillow rocked in the air above Westman's head to the beat of Duncan's heart.

Westman opened his eyes again and looked at the young man, as if to ask, *What are you waiting for?* This man who a minute ago was about to die wanted, really wanted, to die.

The brick-filled pillow grew even heavier, and Duncan dropped it back to the bed next to the man.

No, Westman would live on, feeding tube in his nose. In the end, Ryder made the selfish choice. He had refused to soil his own conscience to help the old man die.

***

This is how the Almighty God believing himself to be a young man named Duncan Ryder first started taking medications for his so-called mood disorder.

How many therapy sessions had Ryder been to? Seemed like hundreds. But this was his first visit to the shrink. The psychiatrist. Da man. Dr. Sanat Ghulati. This guy had the power to prescribe medicines or to have him committed to the hospital against his will.

He expected things to go very much like his therapy sessions with the intern psychologist, but he was nervous going in just the same.

Before the appointment, Duncan had read the little card he'd been given. "4:30 p.m. Tues., Feb. 3, '97 w/ Dr. Sanat Ghulati." This part was handwritten by his therapist last week. The card was preimprinted with the address of the Community Mental Health Clinic.

He looked at the first name again. Sanat. He'd never heard that name before. "Could be rearranged to spell 'Satan,'" he said out loud.

"Or 'Santa,'" a voice said from nearby.

The waiting room had been empty. Someone must have come in without him hearing.

Sanat Ghulati was of Indian descent. Roughly fifty to fifty-five. Short and nearly bald. His skin was just dark enough to hide any redness he may ever otherwise have to show his embarrassment, if he ever felt it. "I'm Dr. Ghulati," he offered. "I am ready to see you now. Please come in to my office."

Dr. Ghulati seized on Duncan's dis-ease by firing questions at the young man as though through a tommy gun, expertly interrupting each answer with the next question with lightning speed, manipulating the pace and the direction of their talk.

He knew Ryder's mind was sharp, but if he was quick enough, he could keep control by never giving him time to second-guess, never allowing him to reflect on the question before he answered.

He sat down silently, and Duncan was invited to take one of the chairs on the other side of the desk. He wondered if the shrink gave any thought to which chair he'd chosen.

The chair closest to the door would show possible desire to flee. The other, cramped and crowded, seemed the choice if he was looking for some shelter or protection from the outside world.

The fact he was aware of the idea each choice conveyed negated the body language of the choice. He had hesitated. And the doctor knew what that meant as well. Or maybe he was just overthinking again, like his therapist had always told him not to.

As he slid into the interior seat, with false bravado, the first question came like a first punch from Mike Tyson. "Are you nervous?"

"Well, yes."

"Why?"

"Because I don't want to be here and I don't know what to expect."

"But you are here and you have expectations."

"Well . . ."

"So what do you expect?"

"Well, I don't know . . ."

"You do know. You just don't want to say because it is your expectation that makes you nervous. What expectation makes you nervous?"

"Maybe that you will talk to me awhile and then tell me I have an unnatural sexual attraction to my mother."

"Do you?" The doctor was smiling slightly.

"Aw shit! THIS is why I am nervous!"

"Do you?"

"What? Have an attraction toward my mother?"

"Yes. A sexual attraction. Do you?"

"Well, yes. But no more than everyone else does."

"Everyone else? Tell me who is 'everyone else'?"

"Everyone has oedipal tendencies."

"Do they? What is that?"

He had turned Ryder into the corner. Now he had to explain basic theories of psychotherapy to a psychiatrist. Twenty seconds or so in the office and the doctor had seized control by surrendering the control to the patient.

"A sexual attraction toward one's mother," Duncan droned. "But it is not unnatural. Everyone has it."

"Yes," the doctor agreed, "we all are sexually attracted to our mothers. It is natural." He apparently said it to set Duncan a little more at ease again. It did not work.

The doctor had said "we." This was disturbing to Duncan. It made him picture the sort of ugly little man and his mother. She would be old. Wrinkled and very ugly. A very unsexy matriarch. He shuddered.

After meeting God face-to-face, years from now, Duncan would understand exactly why everyone was attracted to their mother.

"It's cold in here," he said.

"You told me you expected me to say you had an *unnatural* attraction to your mother. What makes yours unnatural?"

Duncan sighed softly. He was starting to feel as though he did not want to get well. He ignored the question.

"I hate you, you know?"

"Of course you do. Do you know why that is?" the doctor asked with more compassion and understanding in his voice than Ryder would have guessed him capable of.

"Yeah," Ryder said. "I don't want to be here to begin with. I resent that I need to ask you for help of any kind."

"Yes?"

"So now that I am here to humiliate myself before you, I want a cure. I want you to hand me a magic pill that will make me feel good all the time. Make me feel well adjusted. But that pill does not exist. You cannot wave a magic wand, and you cannot fix me. So I personify my frustration in you and so I hate you."

Dr. Ghulati, the man of the tommy gun questions, paused a long while. He looked up at Duncan and said simply, "That's exactly right."

***

This is how the Almighty God operating in the form of the Prophet Elias Parker, accidentally introduced Tylee Christiansen to the love of her life.

The Fruit of the Loom underpants seemed to be dancing all by themselves. Their owner, whose name was printed in the back of them in black laundry-proof magic marker, was dark as the night in which he danced.

A moon dance, the Prophet called it, even though Ryder saw no moon. No moon and no stars through the thick shroud of clouds.

The black magic marker did not say "the Prophet" since they would not return to him from the laundry if they did. The magic marker read "Elias Parker." Duncan would learn to call him the Prophet much later.

Elias liked Duncan. He always did what was asked of him when Duncan did the asking. The rest of the nursing staff could just go to hell for all he cared, and that was why Duncan was out in the icy air now instead of rushing in from the cold as he would very much like to do.

He was there to bring the "nutcase" back indoors. No one else would have been able to get him in without the use of force.

"Elias, what on earth are you doin'?" Ryder asked, closing the car door and trotting through the darkness toward the skinny black man and his underpants.

"Just a little jig. A little moon dance," the blackness above the underpants replied.

Duncan sang now (Van Morrison): "It's a marvelous night for a moon dance."

"It is!" agreed the prophet with big white teeth now showing in a full grin.

"Know what, buddy?" Duncan asked as he came to a stop next to the dancing underpants.

The Prophet stopped and breathed heavily, smokelike steam coming from his whole face, which was still grinning. "What is it, my dear friend?"

"That song was about October skies, and this is December, dude."

"You shittin' me, man?"

"Swear to God. And there is no moon out tonight either."

The Prophet's eyes squinted at the sky. "Are you sure, my friend?"

"Without a doubt, my friend," Duncan replied. "It may even start to snow before we can get back inside."

"It is cold enough to snow," he said, and then he stood straight up, his eyes closed, as Duncan slipped his own brown leather jacket over the man's narrow shoulders.

If Duncan had known then that Elias was a prophet, he would have been in awe of this moment. "It will snow!" the Prophet stated. "In about three more minutes."

"Well, we better get inside before it does, hadn't we?" Duncan said and gently touched the Prophet's shoulder, shepherding him back to the warmth of Cheney Home, where half the nursing staff was watching them from through windows and glass doors.

***

This is how the Almighty God, living the life of a psychiatrist named Sanat Ghulati, began to suspect he had his patient, Duncan Ryder, on the wrong medications.

Ryder: "So I'm sitting in the movie theater and it's crowded, right. I'm watching *The Matrix*. Did you see it?"

"No."

"Well, you should. It kicks ass. I don't know. I actually feel that way a lot."

Ghulati: "What way?"

"Well, in the film, see, he finds out his whole life is unreal. The world is an illusion. A computer program—"

"A computer program?"

"Yeah, you have to see it to understand, I guess."

"So you feel your life is just a computer program?"

"No, I mean I guess, kind of. Listen though. This guy, who later turns out to be the bad guy, has this line. He says something like 'Why, oh why, didn't I take the blue pill?' and—"

Ghulati interrupted. "Pill? He's in a computer program and wondering about what pills he should take? You are taking all the medicines I am prescribing for you, aren't you?"

"Yeah, of course. That's not the point, really. He is living in the real world at the time," Ryder paused. He was trying to see where the doctor was taking the discussion, but still felt it was his time and he should be the one to control what they talked about.

"You know what, Doc? You may have a point in this. I am not sure I want to live in the real world either. And the hero doesn't seem cut out for the real world. He hooks back into the computer to free everyone else. They call him 'the One,' but he could easily have been called 'Messiah' and the whole movie would have made just as much sense. But I'm really trying to tell you about how when the bad guy says this line to the hero on screen . . ."

"The 'Why didn't I take the blue pill' line?"

"Right. See, the blue pill is offered to him with a red pill. The blue pill will put him to sleep, and he wakes up believing he just dreamed it all. The red pill takes him out of the Matrix."

"The Matrix is the computer program?"

"Yes. So when he says 'Why didn't I take the blue pill?' he is wishing he had continued to live in the Matrix."

"The fake world."

"Yes. When he said that, my eyes started to tear up, and I choked down a sob, you know? I could tell other people could hear me. I could sense their disdain. It was like they were silently mocking me for being choked up by this movie, right?"

"Yes? Did anyone say anything?"

"No, but I could feel people's discomfort with me and my emotions in the theater, and—"

"So they can say, 'Hey, it's only a lousy movie,' but you can't help it. And they don't see the irony that their own life is really no more meaningful even though the movie you are watching is showing the world as a mere illusion."

"I think you really did see that movie, Doc."

"No, Duncan, but I think I am starting to understand you a little better than you would like to give me credit for. And please stop calling me 'Doc' before I start referring to you as 'that wascally wabbit,' agreed?"

Ryder laughed. "Deal."

"Duncan, I want you to try to realize that you probably imagined their disdain because you were probably not actually feeling someone else's emotions. Just your own."

"Right. You are always telling me that I can't feel for someone else."

"But it is just a feeling in YOU that you project on those around you. They probably did not even notice you crying because they were watching the movie too."

"Okay. I am willing to accept that as a possibility."

"Our time's almost up for today, do you have something more to say?"

Duncan had protested being cut off at the end of their time so abruptly in the past, and the man of the tommy gun questions was conceding to give him a five-minute warning now. This was his one and only chance to make his final thoughts known succinctly and wrap up the session.

"Well, Dr. G.," he began his closing statement, "I wanted to say that sometimes I have been feeling such a detachment to the world around me that I feel no sorrow whatsoever for real events. War breaks out, or a neighbor or a close friend dies even, and I don't feel sorrow. I feel no pain. I stand there like Superman with bullets of sorrow bouncing off my chest, and I just keep grinning."

"But something fictional makes you sob uncontrollably?"

"Yes, a book, a movie, a song, or just something, you know, something trivial . . ."

"Or like the line about the blue pill?"

"Yes, something that small, like a joke made by a fictional character, brings out my waterworks. The trivial is my kryptonite."

"The devil is in the details," Ghulati offered.

"Huh? Well, kind of. But that's not really what I meant. I've had this recurring dream where I am trying to save people from a world that is not real. I keep dreaming of reincarnating and bringing people 'through' with me."

"Is it a recurring nightmare?"

"I don't wake up screaming, but usually sweaty and breathing loudly and stumbling for a glass of water. Does that count as a nightmare?"

"I'd say so. Still have them with the Prozac?"

"More so, but my dreams have *always* been very vivid like that."

"Prozac should reduce that."

"Really? It doesn't seem to be working as expected then."

"So bringing people through with you to reincarnate . . . ?"

"Yes, but it is like a rescue. I'm not murdering people, even in my dreams."

"Good to hear."

"Well, I do have other nightmares where I am violent. Abhorrently violent. I once dreamed a doorman at a bar wouldn't let me in, and I snatched his wooden stool out from under him and beat his skull with it until his brains were oozing out onto the pavement."

"Really? Was this recent?"

"No. That was before the Prozac."

"Okay, you said a close friend died? Who died recently?"

"I, uh, I don't really want to talk about that. And I'm sure we are out of time now anyway."

"Okay, okay. So we are." The doctor wrote out an illegible prescription as he muttered, "Saved by the bell this time, huh?"

"You know, Doc . . . DOC-TOR . . . I have never known you to use so many clichés." Ryder chuckled as he reached out to take the prescription being held out to him.

"And I," the doctor retorted, "can't remember you comparing yourself to Superman or a messiah so many times before."

"Touché."

***

This is how the Almighty God, believing herself to be a paraplegic named Tylee Christiansen, came to meet the love of her life.

Tylee watched through a window as a pair of underpants seemed to dance by themselves in the cold night air. The nursing staff all huddled around the windowed front of Tylee's new home watching the dance of the underpants. They were muttering to one another.

"Damned crazy loon!" one of them said.

"Hey, Duncan's here early!" another one shouted out. She pointed to the long-haired young man who was stepping out of a silver Toyota Corolla with rust spots all over it. "He will get him to come inside. Just you watch."

The nurses had all tried to persuade the self-proclaimed moon dancer to return to the warmth of the indoors. One by one, they had all failed to persuade him and came back inside, head hung low, and deferred to one of their peers, who failed just as badly.

Tylee did not hear a word that was said by the long-haired man in white, but she saw the jacket appear to dangle above the underpants and saw them walk her way next to the white uniform that turned out to have a pretty handsome guy inside of it, now that they were close enough for her to see him.

The guy smiled widely as the two men came in from the cold night air. "Good thing I got here early," he said.

"Sure is!" exclaimed the nurse who had been the first to return without Elias in tow. She was also the one who had called him a crazy loon. This had bothered Tylee.

Elias laughed loudly. "It's cold out there!" He grinned.

The nurse who'd predicted Duncan would bring the wayward moon dancer inside stepped forward and wrapped a blanket over the smiling man as Duncan removed his coat from the Prophet's shoulders. "Well, duh!" She laughed. "Let's get you to your room and get some clothes on you."

"You go with Bev now. All right, buddy?" Duncan smiled.

"Okay." The Prophet shivered with an undying grin.

The nursing staff huddled around the blanket-wearing man and ushered him down the hall.

The long-haired man stood in the doorway and put his jacket back on. He looked over at Tylee who abruptly realized she was staring at him. "Hello," he said, reaching out to her for a handshake. "I'm Duncan Ryder. I work the night shift here. You must be the new girl they told us was moving in today. Kylie, is it?"

"Tylee," she corrected and took his hand.

***

Tylee wheeled herself into the dining room where Ryder had just begun his lunch break.

"I couldn't sleep," she lied.

The truth was that Duncan Ryder sustained her. She adored him, his laughter, and his way of treating her like an equal and looking past her disability. Most of all, she loved his spirited and passionate conversations that made him seem so much like her father.

She could not exercise her legs anymore, so she loved to talk with Duncan and exercise her mind.

Duncan had a way of making her see the world in grand new terms. He was smart, and he challenged her to think and learn. And he was funny, making her feel relaxed, open, and joyful.

He was also cute.

Tonight, she noticed for the first time that Duncan had a tattoo. The bottom half of a yin-yang symbol was showing beneath his sleeve.

"You have a tattoo!" she exclaimed. As soon as she spoke, she knew she had shown a bit too much enthusiasm. She was not particularly fond of body art, but everything about Duncan made her feel like sunshine.

"Oh yeah." Duncan blushed a little. He raised his sleeve enough to show the whole tattoo. Tylee swooned at his toned bicep, but he didn't notice and quickly pulled the sleeve back down again.

"I, uh, I had to prove I was cool in my younger days, and, well, it's just one of the many things I would change if I could go back and do it all again."

"Are you a Taoist?" She was proud she knew to pronounce the *T* as if it were a *D*.

"Naw. I was just kind of fascinated with the idea of good and evil being part of each other. Not enemies, but in harmony, you know?"

"Yeah, I like that too. But you don't feel that way anymore?"

"Well, sure. I just wish I had not chosen to advertise a religion on my arm. I'm agnostic, you know."

"So what else would you change if you went back in time? Besides forgoing any ties to religion?"

"Oh hell, Tylee. I don't know." He sighed. "I'd like to tell you something sage like a Zen master. Like maybe 'All that has brought me to this plane is good because it has brought me here.' But you and I would both know I was just talking bullshit."

She had gotten him started, now she could smile and nod, and he would entertain and enlighten her for hours—or until his break was over, anyway.

"I mean," he went on, "I know I would change things if I could. For one thing, I'd go down to Kansas City and stop you from driving home that night."

She really liked that his first thought was to help her change something in her past instead of his own, but she interrupted anyway.

"But if I'd never had that accident, we would never have met."

"But we have met! We have to have met, or I would not have known where to go to save you."

"But I would not know you then. Maybe I wouldn't listen to you."

"Maybe I'd have to force you."

Tylee laughed. "You and what army?"

"I don't know. How about the Salvation Army?"

"So you'd all line up along I-70 in Santa suits and ring your bells to warn me off the road?"

"Ho, ho, ho!" he boomed. "Anyway, it's senseless to think about what I would change."

"Why?" she prodded, really wanting him to continue.

"Well, I don't believe in God. So that means I don't believe in time travel."

"How does that follow? My dad believes in time travel."

"Then he must believe in God."

"No. Science is his god. He says so all the time."

"There you have it! He's a scientheist." Duncan laughed.

"There's no such thing."

"Scientologist, then."

"That's not the same thing."

"Sure it is. Well, sort of." He smiled.

"Why do you think you have to believe in both or none?" Tylee asked to bring him back to the point.

"Well, Ty, think about this. If I went back in time and stopped you from getting into that car, I would have thereby changed your existence."

"Yeah, so?"

"And I would be the only one with any knowledge of what I had done. Your life would continue, and you would never realize how I'd saved you from a life in this wheelchair." He lightly kicked her wheel to punctuate his words.

"So?"

"So isn't that what God does? He meddles around in our lives for our own good and never shows his face. He never answers for his crimes, and we just assume it's all for the good because God is good."

"So you're saying you're a god?"

"Well, if I am transcending time and changing other people's destinies, then I am a god, aren't I?"

"So time travel makes you a god . . ."

"No. But if time travel is ever possible, then it has already happened. And that means this sorry-ass world is the best the time travelers could manage."

"Then there must not be a god. Because God would do a better job."

"Maybe. Or maybe he just doesn't want to clean up our messes." Duncan smiled. "But I still contend that my existence is real. My memories are real. There is no one who can change the realness of my own past. If there was, then they are by definition 'God.' They would have authored my reality. They would have created me. Created life."

Both paused for a moment, and Duncan drew in a deep breath. "I would observe the creation of life itself if I could go back in time. Who gives a shit about me and my life? I'm just dust in the wind, right?"

"I care about you and your life, Duncan!" she protested.

"Yeah, but, Ty, you and I are both just insignificants. If I could travel through time, I would not change things. I'd just watch the one who did. I would spy on God. I would go back to the origin of life and see how he did it."

"And you would tell him he's an idiot and that you don't believe in him because you're an atheist," she volunteered.

"Agnostic. I haven't made up my mind yet."

"So what if you could go back but your doubt was confirmed? What if there is no God and life was just an accident?"

"Well then, as the only witness to the primordial soup's recipe, I would become God," he boasted.

"How?"

"Well, life witnessing the beginning of life and having the power to stop it but letting it happen—that's creating it."

"That doesn't follow."

"Sure it does. If you saw your accident was about to happen, you would never have gotten behind the wheel. If you knew it was going to happen but made the choice to let it happen anyway, then it was no accident!"

"Let's go back to the primordial soup. THAT accident was a long time ago, and it gave me the chance to live and to walk in the first place. The second accident is the one that took it away from me."

"Okay. We're at the soup," he conceded. "But it's not a pool of organic soup."

"It's not?"

"Nope. Boiling saltwater and flat crystal surfaces at the bottom of the ocean coming from volcanic vents."

"And you know this because you were there with God?"

Actually, he was there with God. He just didn't know it yet.

"No," he said. "I read a theory by a German biochemist, and it makes sense. Sort of."

"Really?"

"Yeah. Günter Wächtershäuser."

"Gunter Watertower?"

"Close enough." Duncan laughed. "He proposed that life began in two-dimensional form on crystal surfaces, chemicals coming together in a way which created an environment where more of themselves could come together. It's called a

THERE GO I

self-catalyzing reaction cycle, and this is basically what all life breaks down into."

"Chemical reactions?"

"Chains of chemicals. DNA. Every cell has a blueprint for us. That's the idea of cloning, to take the information from our DNA to remake the whole."

"But this doesn't mean you have to be a theist to believe in time travel," Tylee protested.

"No, but if I could travel back in time and plant a tree before life evolved, then I would become the creator of life. And isn't that the definition of God?

"If people are mucking up time, then some force or personage must be governing time travel. 'Time cops,' so to speak, or at the very least some kind of natural law which keeps people from messing around with destiny for their own gain or profit or amusement."

"I guess that kind of makes sense," Tylee conceded. "You know, I really want you to meet my dad."

"Why?"

"I think he could change your mind. Persuade you."

"Can he travel through time?"

"He's done it. Well, sort of."

"Mmm, hmm. And did he speak with God?"

Tylee laughed. "Not yet, I suppose."

"We all speak with God." The Prophet smiled, who seemed to just appear in the room at that moment.

"Mr. Parker, what are you doing out of bed at this hour?"

The Prophet grinned. "And you will meet him soon."

"Not too soon, I hope," Ryder said, standing. The Prophet had a way of sending chills down his spine, and tonight was no exception.

Duncan pulled out a chair, and Elias Parker sat down.

"So, Mr. Parker," Duncan continued, "you know God, then?"

"Surely, my friend!"

"Is he a Republican?"

"I don't know," the Prophet frowned. "Possibly so. He works for the CIA."

Now Duncan and Tylee both laughed.

"If God is CIA," Duncan said, smiling, "is the devil in the Posse Comitatus?"

"The what?" Tylee asked.

"That's an antigovernment group that refuses to pay taxes, and they won't recognize the authority of the federal government."

"Oooh, scary."

"Yeah. And they have guns too."

"Lots of guns," the Prophet affirmed.

A beep sounded from the nurse's desk, and a light came on outside a room down the hall.

Duncan and Tylee looked down the hall toward the light. The aides still on duty were already answering lights of their own.

"Robert's room," Tylee noted dryly. "He can wait!"

"Hey! Now, I wouldn't make you wait!" Duncan said.

"Yeah, but he's an asshole!"

"Judge not that you be not judged, my friend," he said, standing again.

"For an agnostic, you sure do quote a lot of the Bible," she complained.

He laughed as he pushed in his chair. "That which hath been is now; and that which is to be hath already been; and God requireth that which is past."

As he walked toward the light at Robert's room, Tylee called after him: "Romans?"

"No," he responded, walking backward so he could face her. "Ecclesiastes."

"Ecclesi-what-now?" Tylee said.

The Prophet grinned at her. "Ecclesiastes, honey," he said.

Duncan disappeared through the doorway down the hall, and Elias said, "Elvis has left the building."

***

When Duncan returned from the doorway down the hall, Tylee smiled brightly and said, "Elvis has returned to the building."

Imitating the King, Duncan sat down, saying, "Thank you. Thank you, very much.

"So, Tylee. Your father traveled through time," Duncan said. And then making air quotes with his fingers, he said, "Sort of."

"Yes."

"Tell me about that."

"He sort of traveled into the future."

This is how the Almighty God, believing himself to be a scientist named Dr. Reginald Christiansen, sort of traveled into the future and unknowingly created the Marisian Rift, making time travel possible.

Christiansen was in his basement laboratory working on his home project, which by contract would be owned by the university he worked for. And being a fan of H. G. Wells, he bravely stood on his enormous platform and turned on his machine for the first time.

Immediately, a giant painted sign appeared on the wall in front of him, reading, "Stop!" It looked just like the traffic sign.

Had he been able to stop, he might have done so in a year or two. The controls were separate from the device itself though, and he'd entered into his PC the precise time for the experiment to end. And that time was twenty-four hours into the future.

His wife and daughter had worriedly placed the stop sign in the view of the time traveler's eyes after they found him unresponsive eight hours into his twenty-four-hour journey.

Instead of time travel, Christiansen had discovered suspended animation; and twenty-four hours after he programmed the pad and stepped upon it, he became aware of the world again with the changes brought by that one day's time.

Those changes included a stop sign and two very worried females. A thirteen-year-old Tylee had tried to call him upstairs for supper and found him on the platform unresponsive. She and her mother surmised what had happened.

"I don't know how to turn it off," said the crying mother to the daughter.

Perhaps in his first experiment the scientist should have used an orange like Maris's team. He was stuck until the experiment came to an end.

While he thought he had jumped to the future, he was suspended into it. A future where his wife and daughter had slept on a cot in the basement while the other kept watch for signs of life from the pioneer in time travel.

But just as he had programmed the platform, it brought him back in twenty-four hours, to the delight of both young women.

"All at once, he breathed in," Tylee said to Duncan, "and my mother ran to embrace him, and I got there a second later and we both wrapped our arms around him.

"Mom made him take every medical test imaginable. To this day, his doctor thinks he turned into a hypochondriac. He even went to see a psychiatrist."

"He probably thought your dad was having delusions," Ryder offered with a chuckle.

"Well, he did not tell anyone what he had done. He told the doctors he may have had a stroke to get an MRI done. I'm not sure what he told the psychiatrist. But surely not that he had invented a time machine."

"Surely not!" Duncan agreed.

"That was before my mother died."

"Well, of course. She was there in the story."

"No, I mean RIGHT before. Dad was still going to his doctor asking for more tests when Mom died."

"How did she die, if I may ask?"

"A car crash. She was literally on her way to pick Dad up from his colonoscopy, and someone T-boned her car, going through a red light."

"I'm so sorry."

Tears rolled down Tylee's cheeks. "I think I was ten times as scared when my accident occurred because at the instant I felt Yoda skidding on the highway, I thought of Mom."

Duncan took Tylee's hand and tenderly stroked it while she used the other hand to wipe away her tears.

"Let me get you a tissue," he said. He started to stand, but Tylee gripped his hand harder and pulled him back down gently. She may be crying, but she was holding the hand of her big crush, and there was no way she was going to let go so easily.

**

Within a month at Cheney Home, Tylee was convinced to steel her nerve and try to seduce the object of her affection.

"Kiss me!" Tylee whispered to the man above her. He had just lifted her into bed from her wheelchair. She often pretended to need his help when she did not so that he would put his arms around her.

"What?" Ryder asked.

"Kiss me!" she said out loud this time.

He bent down, considering her request. She put her hands around the back of his neck and pulled him down. Before he even knew what was happening, her tongue was tickling inside his mouth.

He pulled away and staggered backward. He sat down in her wheelchair and exclaimed, "Wow!"

"Are you mad?" she asked, coyly biting her lip.

"Mad? No. But . . . what was that, exactly?"

"Well, I call that a kiss. Did you like it?"

"Um. Well, yes. It's just that—"

"I liked it too," she interrupted. "Come here and do it again."

"I . . . I can't," he stammered. "I have to work. Hazel needs me."

"Maybe I need you too."

He stood up and held up a finger to her. "Hold that thought," he said. Then he left her room and turned toward room 204, where the call light was on above the door.

Ryder left the call light outside her room lit when he arrived in Hazel's room. He took her pulse again: 156 beats per minute. Her hands were hot. She sucked on her oxygen mask like an eager child with candy.

He waited there with her. Waited for something: for a nurse to answer the call light, for the priest to arrive, for the woman's imminent death.

Death is not a word that is used in a place like Cheney Home. The nurses told him on many occasions to say "expiration" in place of "death." To Ryder, expiration is the date stamped on a milk carton. If it wasn't used in time, he would dump it down the sink. Hazel had no date stamped on her, but if she did, it would probably be today's date.

At 4:00 a.m., Hazel first asked the nursing staff to call her family and her priest. But the head nurse didn't want to wake anyone up. Besides, Hazel had begun to relax a little, and her chest pain seemed to subside. The gurgling sound in her throat had become quiet.

It was 7:00 a.m. now, and Duncan clocked out of his shift, but he immediately returned to the second floor to Hazel's nursing station. Her light was still lit, which meant no one had even gone in to check on her or else they had shut off her light and she pulled the string to turn it on again.

"Has anyone called her family?" he queried at the nurse's desk.

It was the shift change. Nurses hate to be bothered at that time when the night shift overlaps with the day shift. During that time, they don't work, they just sit and talk. So they draw the time out as long as possible, throwing in gossip with the medical reports. They just ignored Duncan.

The day-shift aides were running about, complaining about how short they were on time. They were wheeling old grouches out to a breakfast that would not be served for another hour or so.

"Has her priest come yet?"

"Oh, he has better things to do!" snapped the cross night-shift nurse.

"Did you tell him she's dying?"

"She's not dying! She's just scared, that's all."

"Did you call her family?" Ryder interrupted. "Did you call anyone at all?"

"Not at seven in the morning! I'm not calling anyone at this hour! And what are you doing here, anyway? You should be halfway home by now!" she scolded without taking the time to breathe.

"I just want to make sure she's all right before I go."

Now the day-shift nurse wore a cross expression as well. "I hope you know I can't give you overtime for this!"

Finding the insinuation that he was there only to receive overtime pay offensive, Ryder took on his own cross tone.

"I'm off the clock!" he barked. "I came back out of compassion, not greed! When you're all finished chatting, pay us a visit in room 204, won't you?"

He turned back toward room 204. He heard the nurses behind him turn to one another not to discuss the medical needs of the residents, but to deride him for his temper tantrum.

He spun around and approached the desk again. The nurses were too startled to say anything and too embarrassed to acknowledge him.

"By the way," he added through clenched teeth, "if you see any goddamned priests about, send them in, won't you?"

Then Ryder hurried to Hazel's bedside. Her head, propped up on half a dozen pillows, turned to see who entered.

"Oh, honey!" she gasped, holding one hand around her oxygen mask and reaching the other out to him.

He took her weak hand in his and held it to his cheek. It was cold and wet.

"Oh . . . Dear . . ." She sighed with a new gasp of air for every word. "I . . . spilled . . ." He looked around before she finished. She had spilled half of the ice water he'd gotten for her earlier. She had tried to pour it on her own.

"Do you want a drink, Hazel?"

"Oh . . . please . . . yes!"

He poured her a fresh glass of water and raised the straw to her lips. She raised the mask and strained to drink. Her eyes closed in a tight, painful frown as she swallowed. Then she waved her hand to let him know she'd had enough.

"You poor dear," he observed. "It hurts for you to swallow, doesn't it?"

She nodded faintly.

"Where's . . . my . . . son?"

It had been three and a half hours since she'd asked the nurse to call him, and he couldn't bear to tell her the whole truth.

"He still hasn't answered the phone."

"Oh . . ." She sighed. "And . . . and . . . my . . . priest?"

"Ssssh. They are still trying," he lied.

She was quiet. She closed her eyes. He listened to the oxygen bubble through the water reservoir, holding her wrist just in case her pulse were to stop.

Duncan looked around her room. Her handsome son stood proudly in a cap and gown inside a little gold frame on her dresser.

He opened the drawer on her nightstand for some napkins to clean up some of the spilled water. The napkins were gone. There were a few clean cups, some straws, and a stray piece of candy. But what caught his attention was a brown string of rosary beads.

He picked up the beads and held them in the light. They were made of wood instead of the cheap plastic he'd seen before.

He wondered if that meant she was more devout or pious than the other patients.

He placed the beads in her hand, and she smiled. "Are . . . you . . . Cath . . . lic?"

His eyes were moist as he shook his head apologetically. She squeezed his hand as though to reassure him it was okay.

"Just a minute," he said.

He ran into the hall and began to ask everyone who could walk and talk, "Are you a Catholic?"

"Lutheran."

"No. Jewish."

"A what? A Catholic? Well, let me see . . . I . . . uh . . ."

"No."

Finally, "Yes. Why?"

"Well, can you come with me for a minute?" he asked the day-shift aide.

"Nope. I got three more people to get out of bed in time for breakfast." She eyed the nurse's desk to be sure she wasn't seen talking to Ryder.

"Well," he pressed, "if you were dying, would you want your rosary beads with you?"

"Oh, sweet Jesus, yes!" She smiled, almost singing.

"Good!"

He turned back toward room 204, and the aide grabbed his arm.

"Go easy on the nurses, kid," she said tenderly. "They've been here a long, long time. They've seen a lot of patients expire."

"Seen a lot of people die, you mean," he said dryly.

"Seen a lot of people die," she echoed in a hushed voice. She gave him a gentle nod and let his arm go. She looked quickly toward the nurse's desk once more and walked away to perform her morning duties.

Ryder rushed back to 204. The room was silent except for the bubbling of the oxygen. Hazel was whiter than the sweat-stained pillows under her heavy head. Her rosary beads, clutched to her heart, rose and fell with her silent breathing.

He bent over and kissed her on the forehead. Her eyes stayed closed.

Just then, the day nurse came in and turned off her call light.

"If you're off the clock, you shouldn't be here," she whined. "You're not family, and visiting hours don't start till after breakfast."

Duncan stepped aside as the nurse came close to check the oxygen flow. She hesitated a moment then went to the door and yelled out.

"Debbie! Debbie, come here and clean up this spilled water before anybody comes in!"

Hazel's eyes opened, and she looked at Duncan, a faint smile coming over her lips. Then they closed again as the nurse came back into the room.

"So, Ms. Svatos," she sang cheerfully, "how about some breakfast? We'll even bring it to you in bed this morning."

Hazel didn't answer, but her hand uncoiled from around her wooden beads, and they slipped to the floor.

"Well, why did you have this in bed with you?" the nurse cried as she bent to pick them up.

Duncan looked to the ceiling, then to the crucifix above Hazel's bed.

"Are you Catholic, Mrs. Arnold?"

"No, why?" she asked as she put the beads back in the drawer of the nightstand.

"Never mind." Ryder sighed, turning away.

He bumped into Debbie in the doorway and heard Nurse Arnold, who was feeling for a pulse in Hazel's arm, say, "Well, what do you know? Just like that, and she's gone. I better go call her family."

***

The Almighty God doing business as a scientist named Dr. Henry Maris was the only one, even on the research team, who really seemed to understand the rift. It is a timeless dimension that opens into our physical universe at varied times and places, centered on Earth.

But Maris really had no real understanding of it either. Well, he had about as much knowledge of the rift as early scientists who taught of the four elements as the building blocks of everything had knowledge of the periodic table.

The single hole, roughly the size of a water molecule, seems to whip around randomly through time and space, and Maris used to describe it as being like the spokes of a wheel, which, when spinning fast enough, allowed you to see right through them. At first, that is all it was used for, to see through to other times and places.

Then Maris's team began to send things through. First a beam of light. Then with the addition of some technology the government called "the Christiansen Project," they began sending through oranges.

Dr. Christiansen was probably the only person who could have understood the rift the way Maris did. But he was not a part of Maris's scientific team. He had invented a device that he called simply "my project," which, when stolen by the United States government, became known as "the Christiansen Project."

Neither Maris nor Christiansen knew how the rift was created. They assumed it was always there since the singularity whipped around through time and space; it was assumed it was a natural phenomenon, one that always was there. But it was actually created the day Christiansen first tried to use his project to travel forward in time.

Shortly after that failed experiment, his wife died tragically, and Christiansen blamed himself and his project. In his grief, he stopped working on the project altogether.

For reasons unknown, a certain man named Elias Parker sometimes saw glimpses into both projects, the Christiansen Project and the top secret Provo Project, leading immortal beings like myself to call him "the Prophet." For other things he saw, Duncan Ryder also began to refer to him as the Prophet.

Only the combination of the technology of the Christiansen Project and the passage through the dark matter singularity called the Marisian Rift created by it could make time travel possible.

What is known of the rift now, in its so-called natural state, is very fragmented. The experiments they performed were witnessed only by Colonel Guinness and the custodian, Eddie Maris, the adopted son of the doctor who discovered it in the first place.

Eddie did not know he was adopted, and Dr. Maris was not completely sure he was not Eddie's biological father. But he was not.

Incidentally, about two billion years ago, I was Eddie Maris. It was that human form of me that caused the time paradox that created life on Earth. An accident for which I may have apologized for at that time by saying, "Well, I'm only human." Call it self-engineering, sabotage, or evolution, but I am no longer that. No, no longer human at all.

As a human believed to be the son of Henry Maris, Eddie knew his father had found a means to view other times and places. He knew that the Christiansen Project had made it possible to travel through the rift and come out at any place or time. More than this, he knew nothing about the nature of the rift or what it could do, so please do pardon the scant details of that failed set of experiments from which I am the only survivor.

Young Eddie was there to clean up the mess after the first few of many oranges were sent through time and came back five minutes later or five minutes earlier as a mess of juice with little traces of pulp.

Three rooms away, the entire staff of the project could smell the citrus, feel the burning sensation in the eyes as the orange materialized as a puddle on the table and a stickiness all around the room.

Eddie was not sure how many times they sent oranges through over his fifteen years there, but this must be why, over two billion years of travel through the rift, it still gives me a burning sensation to the eyes and the taste of citrus.

***

The Almighty God, believing himself to be a young man named Eddie Maris, was working as a custodian, but not an ordinary custodian. He had to have security clearance to clean up what seemed to be mostly mutilated oranges at a top secret military installation, located beneath a mountain in Utah across a lake from the city of Provo. He had to live on the base and was not allowed to leave during his off hours.

His father got him this job, and at least he was with family here. Most workers at the installation had no family, and those who did have family did not get to see them very often.

He did not understand why he had to clean up splattered orange juice every night, but his father knew very well. The experiments with oranges had been carried out for a couple of years now.

At first, they were peering through the rift to gain information, but now, having stolen some technology from a researcher at Stanford University, they had enhanced their control of the rift and were able to send through objects from one room to another.

The obvious next step with a singularity that bounced between time and space was to send an object to another time as well as another place. And mutilated oranges began appearing in the receiving room precisely five minutes before the equipment sent the corresponding whole orange from the device that resembled a coffee mug warmer in the sending room.

Dr. Maris once joked that they had found the world's most expensive and elaborate juicer. From that day forward, the Marisian Rift was often referred to as "the juicer."

Things began to change when the juicer first sent through a whole orange, apparently unharmed, and arriving precisely five minutes before the equipment sent it from the other room.

Soon, they were making larger "holes" into the rift. Not long thereafter, the first sheep was sent five minutes into the past. Then another was sent five minutes into the future.

On Saturday, August 25, 2001, Dr. Henry Maris planned to step into history, literally. He was to walk five minutes into the past, arriving precisely five minutes before he stepped into the rift in the sending room.

When he arrived in the receiving room, Eddie was waiting to greet him as if he had been waiting at the airport for him to get off the plane.

Maris seemed disoriented and was raving like a crazy man.

"I was not alone!" he cried.

"Not alone," he repeated, rubbing his eyes. He grabbed his son in an embrace that was unnatural somehow. "Come on," he said loudly. "You have to come with me!"

"What? No!" Eddie protested.

"Elvis!" Maris cried. "You were in there with me and Elvis."

Maris was pulling Eddie from the room with such an unexpected force that he did not resist, but went with him into the next room. There they startled the Maris from Eddie's present and Maris's past and future.

He was waiting to enter the juicer at just the right moment. Colonel Guinness sat at the computer terminal giving the countdown.

"Three minutes now," he was saying as the door flew open and father and son burst into the room. The doctor's eyes went wide, and he took a step backward. No one knew what would happen if they touched one another, and he did not want to find out.

"It's Elvis, I tell you!" the doctor yelled. Guinness stood up, but too late. The new doctor pulled his son with him into the juicer.

The doctor that remained in the sending room looked at Guinness, mouth gaping. "What do I do?" he asked, in a clear panic. "Do I go in at the end of the countdown?"

Guinness thought for just a moment. "You have to go," he theorized, "or else we will have a paradox. You already showed up in the other room."

"Are you sure?" the doctor asked, fear in his voice.

The colonel sat back down and replied, "Two minutes, thirty seconds."

"Right." The doctor tried to calm his heartbeat. He took a deep breath, then began almost panting, and lined up with the joined singularities. Preparing to run in and through to the other side, he steeled his nerve and said, "Ready."

But when the moment came, he was not ready; something degraded in his mind, and he forgot why he was there.

"Go now!" the colonel shouted at the precise second planned. The stupefied doctor immediately obeyed. He ran from the room through the door instead of the open rift.

Confused, Guinness stood. He looked at the door that closed behind the fleeing Maris and then he looked into the juicer. The portal to another time and place faded rapidly into the thin air, leaving him alone in a room now empty.

***

This is how the Almighty God doing business as a colonel named Todd Guinness reacted to the paradox of Dr. Maris pulling Eddie into the juicer and the Maris with him in the future fleeing the room that fateful morning.

"You told my father in this very office that you would be able to find Saddam Hussein with this thing. In all this time, you haven't been able to even do THAT."

"That's right, Mr. President. The project suffered a tragic level of failure when we tried to send Dr. Maris through to the past. We had a major paradox," Guinness admitted.

"And now that I need you, you say you can't put my agents on those planes to prevent the attacks?"

"I'm sorry, Mr. President. We just don't have the capability at this time."

"Well, I talk to God, Colonel. And I believe he's telling us to stop trying to be like him. I'm pulling the plug on your project. I believe that's what God wants me to do."

Maris spoke up then. "God is already in the rift. He controls it."

"Yes, Doctor. Playing around with time is God's business, not ours," said the man who listened to the voice of God.

"But, Mr. President," Guinness pleaded, "we've had great success in the other branches of our rift research."

"Other branches?" Maris had no idea what they had been using his rift to accomplish.

Guinness held up his hand to silence Maris. It worked.

"I've seen the reports. I agree there is some great potential there, but the attempts to travel through time stop now. Is that clear?"

"Yes, Mr. President. But I have already found a researcher I believe can replace Maris."

"Fine, but put him on the Mars project."

"Mars project?" This was the first time Maris had ever heard of the Mars project. Guinness raised his hand again.

"But that researcher is Dr. Christiansen, out of Stanford."

"The inventor of the Christiansen Project?"

"Yes, sir."

The man known as "W" paused a moment then reaffirmed what his gut had told him earlier. "No, the Marisian Rift is closed for travel for the time being."

He thought he had made a clever joke by saying "for the time being," but Guinness would not have laughed even if it had been a witty remark.

"Yes, Mr. President," he said.

"Now, I have another meeting I have to prepare for. If we can't stop nine eleven from happening to begin with, by God, we are going to make sure it doesn't happen again!"

"Yes, Mr. President. Thank you for seeing us." Guinness grabbed Maris by the elbow and led him out of the Oval Office.

When Maris seemingly lost his marbles, Colonel Guinness figured it was due to the fact that he did not enter the rift, but did come out. It was a giant of a paradox to be sure.

In fact, Maris's brain was damaged in San Francisco during the Summer of Love, where he was convinced, by the devil, not to go down that street, not to call on that cute girl that he'd met last week. Her name was Denise.

Only Guinness knew they had stolen the Christiansen Project from a scientist at Stanford. His solution was to replace his damaged doctor with the one from Stanford. Of course, he would claim his team came up with the Christiansen Project independently.

So Colonel Guinness would never come to save the Marises. They were stranded in the Summer of Love until they could find their own way out.

***

This is how the Almighty God believing himself to be Eddie Maris was stranded in the past with the man he believed to be his father.

As his father pulled Eddie into the rift that August morning, he was scared and reluctant, even unwilling. The moment he crossed the threshold into the rift, his eyes began to burn from a sort of miasma of citrus, but at the same time, he felt an inexplicable sensation of home. For Eddie, the rift was like his mother's womb.

While he was inside the rift, there was suddenly no other place he had ever known. Had he ever known any scent but orange oil? Had he ever known any place but here? And yet he was not alone. His father still held him tightly. He strained to open his eyes in the acidic atmosphere.

As if in a dream, he saw with his mind, not his eyes, what surrounded him. Sure enough, there was Elvis.

Wait . . . Elvis?

And then it was over, he came out into a dirty back alley. He had no idea where or when he was, but they were definitely in an alley, with a row of tin trash cans and a pile of empty boxes lying around.

Dr. Maris let go of his son and started to stumble. Eddie did not feel dizzy, but obviously Maris did, and Eddie stepped up and caught his father as he began to fall. He gently laid him down in the alley and pulled a small cardboard box over and put it under the man's head like a pillow.

"What . . . ?" Eddie began. "What just happened?"

"Don't you know?" Maris said, looking up at him from his spot on the ground.

"I mean, you just took me through the juicer, right?"

"Yes."

"So where are we?"

"I don't know, Ed. You brought us here."

"Me? That's ridiculous!"

"You is the master of the rift."

Eddie looked down at his confused father, less concerned with being told he was the master of anything than he was with the improper grammar.

"Dad, I think maybe you hit your head or something. Do you feel okay?"

"Fine. I's fine. But I could not hold you still in the rift. There is too many of you in there."

Eddie looked around as if he would see other versions of himself around somewhere. "Are you . . . Are you seeing double or something?"

He waved a finger in front of his prostrate father. "How many fingers am I holding up?"

"Eddie, are you okay?" Maris asked. "Did you forget how to count?"

Eddie had to stop and think. He counted in his mind to ten; then he laughed. His father must be joking.

But Maris was not joking. Not at all. The same thing that had caused Dr. Maris to run from the room instead of through the hole to the rift caused this man before Eddie now to forget—almost everything he once knew.

Yet somehow . . . He seemed to have some new supernatural understanding of the rift. For Eddie had indeed become the master. Just . . . not . . . yet.

This Eddie was clueless. Clueless and stranded in god knows where.

"Well." Eddie sighed. "I suppose that Colonel Guinness will know how to find us. Right?"

"Eddie!" Maris sat up. "Son, you's the only one who can find you."

This made no sense to Eddie at the time, but at least now he was sitting up. "Are you feeling better? Can you stand up?"

"If you wish it," Maris said, standing, less like a newborn colt and more like a just-sprung jack-in-the-box.

Since it seemed they were on their own somewhere in the real world, Eddie decided to look around to try to piece together just how deep a predicament they were stuck in.

As soon as they came out of the alley, Eddie recognized the familiar surroundings of Chinatown, a small part of San Francisco, the city he grew up in years ago.

He had no idea right then that he would spend a much more significant part of his adult life in San Francisco as well. And this time, he would get to experience the Summer of Love.

***

The Almighty God, believing himself to be a rather fat man who has been taking barbiturates risks more than overdose or heart attack. This man in particular did not have the strength to reason. He was about to die, but he did not know it yet.

The man, called the king, sat on his toilet in his home called Graceland. A wicked pain shot into his chest and then into his head, just behind the ears.

His senses whirled, and he fell forward toward the tiled floor. He did not hit the floor. Instead, he fell into a sort of a weightless, drifting roll.

He was in a place where he had no feelings of pain in his chest or his head, just a burning in his eyes and the taste and smell of . . . of oranges.

A voice that was his, but he did not say it (or did he?), now echoed in the weightless void. "Ladies and gentlemen," the voice said, "Elvis has left the building."

***

Christiansen's conditions for joining the Mars Project, the remaining branch of the Provo Project, included bringing his daughter and her caretaker with him. There was no way he was leaving his daughter in California when he was under a mountain in Utah.

Christiansen developed his project without ever discovering the rift, which is what made it work. He would not try to sell or market it, as Tylee had suggested, because he was not sure what he had stumbled upon, and he still blamed his failed project for his wife's death.

Maris did not understand the Christiansen Project either, but he did know that it manipulated the dark matter singularity that he called the rift. It gathered together the tiny holes into the rift around a central location.

When gathered around an object, say, an orange, the effect Christiansen discovered was a sort of time suspension. The orange would not degrade, rot, dry up, or even soften.

Its effect was like a deep freeze without the freezer burn that comes from cold storage. And there was no thawing-out process.

Guinness chose not to tell how Maris had used the same device, which Guinness essentially stole from the patent office, to send oranges back and forth through time. After all, the time experiments had already fried the brain of one brilliant scientist.

Instead, Christiansen was told that the interest in his device was to develop it for space travel. And indeed the project would move to space one day, though Christiansen would only be involved in the experimental stages of the project, the underground research.

What Christiansen thought was a failed experiment in time travel was actually a successful experiment in suspended animation. Christiansen's use of the device had been explored by the team at the Provo Project on a grand scale. There were massive warehouse-sized rooms filled with the little platforms.

One such room was called the ark. Years before, many animal species with dwindling populations were collected in the form of frozen embryos. At "the ark," they were not frozen, but embryos were preserved at room temperature with the Christiansen Project platforms.

Some small animals were preserved as adults. There were mice, for example, live specimens frozen in time. And honeybees that were dying above in alarming numbers were preserved in the ark. Whole hives of them were kept in perfect stasis.

Another room housed seeds and spores of every imaginable kind. They called that room "the Orchard."

If GMO seeds took over all of agriculture, but led to some disastrous famine, there were generations' worth of organic seeds underground in the Orchard that could save the world. Of course, the collection also included the genetically modified seeds as well.

In another section, they were working on medical technologies using the rift. Because of his medical background, Ryder was assigned to work there with research animals.

The head of that small department was an enormous black man. His name was Odin Parker. Duncan didn't know at the time, but Dr. Parker was a cousin of the Prophet, though they had never met.

Dr. Parker had lost his hearing as a teen and was now completely deaf, which had dashed his dream of working in the space program, where astronauts communicated with Earth through radio.

So he worked underground, tirelessly developing the technology that would one day put life on Mars.

When Ryder and the Christiansens arrived, Dr. Parker was working on using the Christiansen Project device and the rift itself as a surgical tool. And he taught Ryder how to take a monkey embryo from a petri dish and implant it in the womb of a female of the species. All this was done with no surgical cutting whatsoever.

This was important to repopulating endangered species, Dr. Parker explained, in detail, in his lab notes. Ryder and Dr. Christiansen studied the notes carefully because neither of them knew American Sign Language, which was Parker's main means of communication. He read their lips when they asked questions and responded in writing.

Embryos still needed a womb in which to form and a mother to be born from.

Parker's plan was to perform the same kind of embryo transplants on elephants at game preserves to protect the species.

It was so easy with the technology they had at hand that even Ryder, trained only as a nursing assistant, could perform the procedure himself.

Ryder and the Christiansens were gradually learning Dr. Parker's American Sign Language as they worked with him by day and studied ASL by night.

One afternoon, Dr. Parker invited the three newcomers to his quarters for wine, crackers, and cheese. He gave them handwritten invitations, one for each guest.

Their quarters were basically small studio apartments with a tiny kitchen area. They had murphy beds and tables that folded up into the wall of the kitchen the same way.

But Parker's quarters were large with a full living room and bedroom and a kitchen. He had apparently negotiated himself a bigger living space when joining the Mars Team. And with seven-foot tall doors, he did not have to duck in his own home.

Even Colonel Guinness had one of the tiny efficiency units.

There was enough space for Parker to give then a grand tour of the place, which he did as soon as they arrived.

"This," Parker said in sign language, after opening his towering bedroom door, "is what I wanted you to see."

Above his king-sized bed (he needed the space since he was so large a man) was a large velvet painting of Elvis. It stuck out from the wall several inches. "I painted this one myself," he signed. "I copied it from a photo of one my parents had."

"Why is it sticking out from the wall like that?" Tylee asked from the doorway. She could not easily fit through the door and into the room with her wheelchair.

"Yeah, are you hiding a wall safe back there?" Ryder added, in sign and speech.

"No, but that's a great question," Parker beamed. He wanted them to ask about that detail.

"It's another experiment I am performing," he said out loud in English. This was the second time they ever heard him speak. The first time was when he told them to call him Odin rather than the more formal Dr. Parker.

"Apparently, Guinness never thought of this application, but I have a small platform back there," he continued.

Duncan noticed that the light on the painting was very bright. It was a sunlamp.

"Half the painting," Odin continued, "is being preserved in stasis, and half is not. And the sunlamp is to fade it over time. I'm going to see if the stasis can preserve the painting from fading or cracking even under strong sunlight conditions."

"So if it works," Tylee said, "then they can use it in museums and galleries and preserve great works of art for generations longer." She also signed, as best as she could, what she said.

"Yes. That's it exactly." Odin smiled.

"But degeneration of a painting takes so long," Tylee said, "How will you be able to check on the results of your experiment?"

"Well," Odin said, "I found with mice that the more I put them in stasis, the longer they lived when taken out of stasis. I think it may actually be the key to combat aging and greatly prolong life."

"That's big!" Christiansen said.

"That must be why Daddy hasn't aged a day in years," Tylee said with excitement.

Odin turned to face the other doctor in the room. "You froze yourself?" he said, amazed.

"Yes. Once," he admitted, giving Tylee a chastising look.

"And she's right," he said. "I have not had a single new gray hair since then."

"How old are you?" said Duncan and Odin in unison.

"I was forty when I froze myself for twenty-four hours. And I was born in nineteen forty-one."

"So you are sixty-one now?" Duncan asked.

"Yes."

"Wow!" Odin exclaimed. "You certainly don't look that old."

Then they shuffled back to the dining room where the wine and cheese were waiting.

"Your little side experiment reminds me of another idea I had," Dr. Christiansen said to Odin. "If you can plant an embryo with no invasive surgery, you could do almost any surgery without a single cut, right?"

"Yes," Odin said. "What did you have in mind?"

Dr. Christiansen gestured to his daughter in the doorway. "She has had several surgeries already, but nothing that can get her out of the chair."

"With this kind of surgery, there would be almost no recovery period, and the surgery would have a greater chance of success," Duncan offered.

Parker nodded.

Christiansen had seen the work on transplants of embryos and immediately saw the opportunity to surgically repair his daughter's spine. Surgery here could be done without any cutting of skin or muscle tissue. It wasn't long after this moment in Parker's living quarters until the three fixed Parker's goal on healing Tylee too.

Of course, their technology could not regrow destroyed tissue. She needed stem cell research, which the government had placed strict limits on.

It was decided that Tylee's cure would have to wait, but for how long? Could she afford to wait any longer with the current restrictions on research?

"Put me in stasis!" she demanded. "When research picks up again, unfreeze me."

They had not yet tried to put a living human in stasis for any length of time longer than Christiansen's twenty-four-hour experiment in his basement, and Tylee and Duncan suddenly were being considered as guinea pigs.

Ryder was frightened a little, but decided that Tylee's happiness was worth the risk.

On Saturday, January 4, 2002, Tylee and her father said their goodbyes, and she and Ryder were put into stasis with Christiansen Project platforms of their own.

"Do you realize this is my thirty-fourth birthday?" Duncan said.

"Stop being sentimental," Christiansen chastised. "Get on the platform."

"Okay, but tell Tylee I love her," the thirty-four-year-old said as he slid into place on the platform.

"Tell her yourself when you wake up."

"But what if I don't ever wake up?"

"You will. I promise."

When he did wake, after a few hundred years, he would not be himself. He would soon divorce himself from his body.

As Duncan prepared for the unknowns of his stasis, lying on his back, he sensed something in the air above him. What he saw was actually a seemingly stray-occurring appearance of the singularity that led to the rift. Convinced he was dying, he thought what he sensed was a passage for his soul to enter. A passage to heaven, perhaps. Maybe there was a god after all.

At that moment, thinking he had died, Ryder's soul and consciousness left his body, which had just been put in stasis, and headed for the light above him. And there he met his destiny.

His eyes did not burn as he entered the rift, like the Marises did. That was because he left his eyes behind in stasis. This was not heaven, though, and Ryder's soul sensed an exit. A hole and his body beneath him.

The body he sensed was his own, but it was not in stasis. Not under a mountain in Utah. It was his body at age thirteen. In a room with a cruddy old orange carpet, he was lazily toying with an innocent beetle that had crawled across that carpet near his school desk.

He went through the narrow opening and headed for his body.

***

This is how the Almighty God, believing himself to be a seventh-grade boy named Duncan Ryder first met the devil, a creature of his own creation.

The gaudy orange carpet was mellowing with dirt and age to a rusty brown color. It had been covering a scratched tile floor of the shithole classroom since long before any of its tired, lazy seventh-grade occupants started kindergarten.

Several students in the classroom were staring at that ugly carpet, some wondering what kind of floor may lie beneath it, some contemplating its rich but dirty color. Most of the class was pretending to take notes on Mr. Woods's lecture, but many were only making doodle marks in their notebooks.

A few others, though, were dutifully jotting down every word coming from the teacher's lips.

Not one of the students dared, however, to gaze out the window to the green, green grass; the blue, blue sky; or the chattering birds that chased one another in a noisy dance of spring. Even a stolen glance out the window would ensure Mr. Woods would interrupt his own lecture with a question.

Then the same kiss-ass note takers would raise their hands, but it would be the daydreamer who would be called upon for an answer. That way, Woods could single out and embarrass the daydreamer, who, if they answered his question wrong, may well be spending their evening at home writing a stupid page from the dictionary.

Everyone hated the dictionary—over two thousand pages of hell it was. As a matter of principle, at least two students per day would be compelled to carry home a volume of that seven-pound torture device. In addition to their homework, they would have to hand copy every last word, symbol, and punctuation mark from a page of that dictionary, whatever page Mr. Woods would randomly call out.

Ryder's vocabulary was now vast, simply from the many times he'd been assigned to carry home the mammoth tome and from all the many pages he had handwritten from it.

On a day like today, a beautiful spring afternoon, Dick Woods (his name a constant subject of whispered jokes and suppressed, guilty giggles) would be grumpy about having to be indoors, just as much as his class was.

Everyone knew that the tiniest infraction today may even earn them two pages instead of just one.

Just last week, the first day after the snow had melted, Woods had assigned out pages to three different students. With all three volumes assigned, he punished the next offender with pages from the Bible instead, as had happened on many occasions before.

"Obadiah chapters 2 through 20, Ms. Goodacre," he said.

Whispers broke out. "Nineteen chapters? That's not fair." Dirty looks were aimed at Duncan from all around the room. He had been assigned the third dictionary, and now he was being blamed for Lisa Goodacre's unfair assignment from the Bible.

Duncan knew the Bible well enough to realize that the book of Obadiah was only one chapter long. Chapters 2 through 20 did not exist, so Lisa was actually receiving no punishment at all. Since he was getting the glares of blame from his classmates, he felt he could not let that unfair double standard pass, and he raised his hand high in the air.

Mr. Woods smiled and looked away with no acknowledgment of Ryder's hand. He turned to face the chalkboard. Duncan's face began to redden. He could feel the heat in his ears. His hand came down, and he blurted out his protest.

"Obadiah is only one chapter long!" he said.

"Hm?" Wood said, turning and raising his eyebrows. "That's true, isn't it?" He mused playfully. "So I guess Ms. Goodacre got lucky."

Lisa smiled.

"You, on the other hand"—Woods smiled—"can add chapter 1 of Obadiah to your dictionary page. What was it? Page 587?"

Laughter broke out throughout the classroom. Duncan could swear, in his humiliation, that Lisa Goodacre had actually stuck out her tongue at him; but when he turned to look at her, she was facing front, hands folded smugly on her desk.

But that was last week.

Today, the snow was gone. The ground was dry, and blades of green grass were showing up all over. In the distance, there was the sound of the first premature lawn mower of the season.

Inside the classroom, it was hot. Hot and boring. No one wanted to listen to Mr. Woods lecturing about the Protestant Reformation. On a normal day perhaps they would listen, but today! Jesus! Today was the kind of day that was supposed to be a Saturday or during spring break.

Today, Mr. Woods was droning on, and Ryder's mind was focused on the rust-colored carpet when a big black beetle caught his eye.

The beetle was crawling across the arid carpet like a camel in a vast desert. When it came near his desk, he stretched out his foot to block the insect's path. It paused then turned to go another direction. He blocked it again. Same result.

He boxed in the little creature this way. He confined the bug to a space between the desks about three feet by two. It was the farthest he could extend his leg into the rows between the desks.

Idly, he drew a doodle in his notebook of a beetle like the one he was playing with. Then the bug grew brave or weary of being toyed with. It scurried up onto Duncan's shoe. His foot rose into the air and violently twitched to dislodge the daredevil insect.

"Mr. Ryder!" Mr. Woods said suddenly. Presumably, he planned to follow with a stock teacher's wise-ass remark. Perhaps something like "Do you have something to share with the rest of the class?"

At that moment, the beetle lost its grip and fell to the floor on its back. The poor thing's legs wiggled and scrambled in the air in a desperate attempt to right itself.

The girl seated next to Duncan screamed a loud, terrified scream. Other students stood up and stretched to see what was happening at Ryder's desk.

Duncan's sneaker came down with a heavy thump onto the helpless little black body. The pandemonium that this distraction provoked could well lead to Ryder's suspension. It did the first time around.

Ryder would think his life had ended with that suspension. He felt he had been squashed just the way he ended the life of the beetle that had done him no harm. And he did it just when the creature was most vulnerable, struggling wildly amid a classroom of screaming and shrieking seventh graders.

But this was Ryder's second time around. At the instant his foot met the ground, he felt not himself. An observer in his own body.

And he was. He had been suddenly occupied. Occupied by his older self. The soul of the Ryder that would later be inserted himself into the body of his young seventh-grade self.

There was a pregnant pause of silence. Duncan looked around the room slowly; all other eyes were on him. No one expected this distraction from the Protestant Reformation lecture, but they could all appreciate any diversion, and this one was about to become much more interesting than any of them could imagine.

"Mr. Ryder!" Woods lowered his chin and cleared his throat.

Duncan looked up with perhaps the widest eyes ever seen on a seventh grader's face. His gaping mouth slowly widened into a smile, but not just a smile, more a nearly insane expression filled with joy and elation.

No one could muster a conceptual reason for such joy on his face. He was about to get assigned a couple of dictionary pages at least and maybe even get detention or suspension.

"Mr. Ryder!" the teacher's stern voice repeated slowly.

Now the whole class heard the grinning young Duncan Ryder loudly exclaim, "Holy shit!" Now they may be watching Ryder's expulsion and not just suspension. Now heads throughout the room turned to face Mr. Woods. None could guess what wrath may issue forth after this incredible and unprecedented course of events.

The piece of chalk in Woods's hand fell to the floor as if he simply forgot he was holding it. In fact, he did forget. Surely, even a troublemaker and class clown would never blurt out what he just heard come from the student before him. But Duncan Ryder had just not only used the s-word right out loud, but he had also done so with a giant shit-eating grin.

What the hell?

He didn't say "What the hell?" of course. Like his class of seventh graders, he was dumbstruck. He stood and stared at Ryder in total disbelief.

"Holy shit!" the boy repeated, slamming his palms on his desktop. "I'm really fucking here!" Both hands gripped the desktop as though it were the only stable object in a spinning room. "This is no dream!" he said.

Woods' room was spinning as well, it seemed, and he fell back and sat on the edge of his desk. He was sure he was not dreaming either. A student had just disrupted his class and had used the f-word right out loud. He struggled for words, but all that came out was just an echo of the last two word he had used: "Mr. Ryder!"

He struggled, but nothing else came out of his mouth for a few moments while Duncan Ryder looked himself over, amazed at his thin young body.

Then he looked around him at the audience of students. The girl next to him, the same girl who had screamed at the upside-down beetle, was now praying feverishly. Her hands were folded and eyes closed in terror. Little whispers were coming from her. She thought she had just witnessed a possession. And she had. The first ever possession by the devil.

"Did you see it?" Ryder cried excitedly. "Did you see me come in? What did it look like?"

Now Woods mastered his confusion enough for words. Words familiar to him already.

"Are you going for a record?"

Those words normally would be followed by pages from the dictionary or the Bible being assigned to some unlucky student. In fact, the record was currently held by Duncan. He had been assigned a page a night for an entire week.

That had been assigned for asking the question "Why do all the non-Christian scientists continue to back each other up in committing such massive fraud?"

Ryder was not trying to be a smart-ass. He really could not understand why they would falsify evidence to support the theory of evolution just to discredit the biblical story of creation.

So now, when asked "Are you going for a record?" Duncan's response was, "I think I've already set a record. After all, here I am!"

Words finally came to Woods now. "Sit down and be silent this instant, or you will break the record for NOT being here!" Actually, though, the boy was already sitting at his desk. But he sure was not silent.

Woods was not sure if he should physically escort the boy from class. While the school policies did allow for corporal punishment, spanking a thirteen-year-old boy would be frowned upon by parents and administrators alike. But he had to do something to regain control of his class again.

"Oh my god!" Ryder screamed. "Rebecca!" Now, he stood and crossed to where Rebecca stood three rows behind him. He threw his arms around the helpless girl. "God, it's so good to see you again!"

Woods jumped to his feet again and barked out, "Duncan Ryder! Take your seat this instant!"

Rebecca Sutton had died in '91 when her abusive boyfriend beat her too hard, hitting her head against a wall.

Ryder, having had a secret crush on her all through grade school and on into high school, would not be so easily persuaded to break his long-belated embrace of the girl he loved for so many, many years.

Now, Woods, through clenched teeth, rebuked him: "Mr. Ryder!" He was marching down the aisle before he got through the name.

"Oh, shut up, Woodsey!" the boy returned.

Woodsey was a nickname the teacher had never heard before. The students used it only behind his back.

The real Woodsey was a cartoonish owl used as the face of an antipollution campaign. He was never as popular as Smokey the Bear, but what Smokey was to forest fires, Woodsey was to pollution. Besides the similarity in name, Mr. Woods had once told a student to clean up his act, prompting the new nickname.

Two giant hands grasped Duncan's wrists and easily pried his arms away from Becky.

Now, corporal punishment seemed like a much better option to the man, and he began to physically usher the boy from the room.

"Let go of me, you son of a bitch!"

Duncan soon realized he was no match for Woods physically, not in his skinny thirteen-year-old body, anyway. Still, he resisted his escort to the door with kicking, pushing, and grabbing at desks.

Then he said out loud, "Wait! I've done it once, and I can do it again!"

Woods could only explain this open insurrection with drugs. It must be marijuana, he thought. This kid was out of his mind and would be expelled for sure.

Duncan actually was expelled, but in the eighth grade, not the seventh. He'd always believed it was the best thing to ever happen to him. He had gotten away from the repressive religious schooling and was no longer punished for asking questions at school. He was finally able to pursue his interests and really learn.

Public schools, it seemed were not so evil, not at all far behind the intellectual standards of Manhattan Christian School, as he had been told since he was in kindergarten.

As Woods was forcing the boy to the door, just a few feet from the goal, he abruptly let go of Ryder's wrists, and Duncan fell limply to the floor. Woods let out an agonized, bone-chilling scream of pain.

His hands clasped the sides of his head and he fell to his knees. He clenched his teeth and swallowed. It was the most intense migraine he could imagine.

Moments later, Woods was lying on the floor next to the motionless body of the boy. Both were still. Were they even breathing?

The entire class crowded around in a hushed circle, looking on in dumb amazement.

Then barely audible, the weak voice of Mr. Dick Woods pronounced the words: "It worked. I'm really here."

***

The frightened seventh graders crowded in tightly around the near lifeless bodies. Mr. Woods's fingers began to twitch, and as if of one mind, the class fearfully leapt backward just a little bit.

"Should," someone stammered, "should we, uh, call for an ambulance?"

A low moan came from the floor: "Noooo." Mr. Woods rolled over and slowly sat up on the floor. A thin trickle of blood decorated his right cheek. It was coming from his ear.

"He's bleeding!" the same student voice called out. "Someone go get Principal Stockton."

"No!" Woods barked with a sudden explosive energy. "No one is to leave this room! I am in control here."

"But you're bleeding from your ear."

Woods wiped the trail of blood with the back of his hand. Then he turned to his hands and knees, and the children, again, jumped back as if with one mind. That one mind seemed to know he would need more space.

"Mr. Woods," came a timid voice. It was Lisa Goodacre. "Are you all right, Mr. Woods?"

"Fine, sweetie, I'm fine."

"But you're bleeding, sir."

He looked at the blood on his hand as he remained with his knees on the floor. "I said I'm fine. Try not being a little suck-up for once, Lisa."

Just a second earlier, he'd called her "sweetie," which made her heart skip a beat. Now he was insulting her, and her heart beat faster with the injury.

The thirteen-year-old Duncan then became aware of the beating of his own heart. The last he remembered was a beetle's legs squirming in the air. Now he was himself lying on the floor. Closer to the door than to his desk. And there was Woods, sitting on the floor next to him with blood smeared across his cheek and on the back of his hand.

Had he fainted? He noticed a pain all over his body, but particularly a bruise on his right shoulder indicated he must have fallen. He raised his sleeve to examine the bruise. It was a new bruise, judging by the color, but it was big.

"Back to your seats, everyone," Woods ordered. "Now, goddamn it!"

Obedient feet pounded the carpet all around Duncan, but he still felt too faint to stand.

Woods struggled to his feet and shuffled to the chair behind his desk at the front of the classroom. "Strong-willed bastard," he muttered.

As the students took their seats, he surveyed the scene. "I wonder . . . ," he mused quietly. "Maybe it's easier on a kid."

Lisa was trying to make sense of the recent events and stared at the teacher to whom she would surrender her heart willingly.

She would one day too. Shortly after graduation, she and Woods would have a brief affair; she would hope, pray, and plead that he would leave his wife for her.

Mrs. Woods, for her part, had astutely felt for years that Woods no longer wanted her; and rather than taking a lover of her own, she drowned her insecurities with food. Since they wed, she had put on over a hundred extra pounds. She was enormous. Her pain was enormous.

Ryder only found out all of this since he entered Woods's head a minute or two ago. Well, he did not know yet of the affair. Woods himself had merely fantasized about it.

What a sicko! thought the Ryder that was now exploring the brain of Mr. Woods. After all, the girl was just that, a girl. Her boobs had not even finished coming in.

After a short silence, Woods's head dropped onto the desk.

The spirit of Ryder forced itself into the mind and body of the girl that had just been staring at him. Lisa Goodacre was much easier than Woods had been. No blood came from her ear either.

"Oh my!" Lisa suddenly exclaimed. "Why, little Lisa! What thought you have! Shame on you."

Woods's head slowly and painfully lifted up. He pulled a Bible from the desk drawer. His whole body shook with weakness and frailty as he raised the Bible up as far as he was able, which was not over his head as he had wanted.

He knew he had been forced aside in his own mind by some sinister force, possessed by a demon, he believed. Until that day, he had believed only a person without Jesus in his heart could be possessed by a demon.

But this was not a demon. With that forceful possession of Woods, the devil himself was born. It was the first time Ryder ever forced himself into the mind and body of another human.

He had entered his younger self first, but that was easy, natural. It was like coming home after a hard day of work. After all, it was his own mind he was invading. The territory was compatible. He had known the password, so to speak. Woods was different though. It was more like he hacked his way in.

Woods felt as though he had been forced to be a passenger in his own mind, tied up and thrown into the backseat while the presumed demon took the wheel. Not knowing it was the devil himself that threw him in the backseat, Woods believed the demon had been working under orders from Satan, so Satan was who he addressed as he held the Bible up over his heart instead of his head.

His raspy voice came out with swallowed fear: "Satan! Satan, I command you in the name of the Lord Jesus Christ to leave this place at once!"

Lisa laughed. "Satan? You think I'm Satan?"

Ryder was still unaware of the role he had cast himself in.

"Jesus said: 'Whatsoever thou looseth on earth is loosed in heaven, and whatsoever thou bindeth on earth is bound in heaven.'" His voice was a little shaky, not only because he had just been possessed by the devil, but because he was not sure where in the Bible that quote came from or if he said it quite right.

More forceful now: "I now BIND you in the name of Jesus!"

"Come and bind me then, you Woody Dick," the girl's voice taunted. "Yeah, I know now just what makes your dick woody, Woodsey."

Lisa's hands pulled up her skirt to reveal her flowered cotton panties. "You like little cotton panties like these, don't you, Woodsey? You little pervert!" her voice said.

"Get thee behind me, Satan!" screamed the trembling man at the head of the class.

He had been sure the demon was here somewhere, but until Lisa spoke up, he did not know where the spirit had gone.

"Get thy needle dick behind this, you pedophilic asshole!" Ryder made Lisa's body spit and turn her back to Woods. She thrust out her butt in his direction.

"Devil!" the weary teacher cried.

"Why not call me something else?" she seemed to say. "Lucifer. Beelzebub, or why not Memnoch?"

"Lucifer!"

"Better," the girl said. "But enough fun here."

Ryder left her body as Lisa sat at her desk. Her body went limp, and she laid down her head on the desk as though napping.

There was a whooshing wind sound through the room, and Duncan's crumpled body sprang to its feet.

"I'm going out to play," he said. "But don't think I'm leaving because of your sorry Jesus voodoo and all that horseshit."

He turned toward the door, which opened for him as if he were exiting a supermarket.

"How 'bout that?" He grinned. "I can do all kinds of shit."

***

As the two Duncans in one body strode confidently toward the open door, there was at once another whooshing sound. All at once, it seemed, a man was standing in the doorway, blocking Duncan's exit.

It was Eddie, an older and wiser Eddie.

"Young man," Eddie said, "we need to talk."

"Who the hell are you?"

"Someone who's come here to help. Help you find the reason you're here. I'm a time traveler, just like you."

"No one on earth is like me!" Duncan sneered. "I can travel through time and space with a mere thought. I can control other people and see their thoughts and memories. I can move things without touching them. And now I have changed my own history."

"Well, you certainly have changed history," the man said as he gestured sweepingly around the room.

The entire classroom was silent. Everyone, even Woods, had their heads on their desks as though napping as Lisa had done at the moment Ryder left her body and mind.

"Let's say there was a gas leak," Eddie said. "They will think they dreamed all of that up."

"The same dream?"

"They have forgotten what just happened and are dreaming their own dreams now."

"How did you manage that?"

"I don't know. You're the one who did it. Or at least you will do it."

Eddie handed over a note. Ryder read it silently. It was a ransom note of sorts. It said if Eddie wanted his son back, he needed to come to this place and this time.

Eddie had thought his beloved soul mate had suffered a miscarriage. But the note said that Ryder had removed the fetus before it could be born, and he had put it artificially into a surrogate mother.

The note also said, "Don't worry. All the witnesses will be unconscious from a gas leak I will cause. Their dreams will erase their memories of us." The note was handwritten in Ryder's own penmanship. It was signed with his name.

"I don't know anything about your son."

"You took him!"

Duncan thought for a second. He did know how to use the technology of the Christiansen Project to take out a fetus and implant it in a surrogate.

After a moment, he said, "If you are truly a time traveler, you must realize that I may have written this note in my own future. Maybe I will take your son. I don't know. But I haven't yet."

"Then why does it say to come here now?" Eddie demanded.

"I don't know. You tell me, Dr. Who. I just got here. This is the first place I came. Did Dr. Christiansen send you the first time?"

"Dr. Maris did."

"Who in the hell is Maris?"

"You're the one who scrambled his brain!"

"Again, something I have not done yet!"

"Wait. Did you say Dr. Christiansen sent you here? The inventor of the Christiansen Project?"

"Yeah, why?"

"Where did you meet him?"

"Stanford. Again, why?"

"It was you that made Dr. Christiansen leave San Francisco. You are responsible for the team first meeting him in the future. The effect came before the cause."

"Whatever. This is all a bunch of horseshit! I'm going out now."

Eddie realized something at that moment, that his consulting with Dr. Christiansen in 1967 had changed the time line. He had caused Christiansen to move to Stanford. He had been the one that drove the inventor out of San Francisco.

"Don't you see?" Said Eddie, "You were not meant to travel through time. I traveled to the past and met Christiansen. When he helped me get back through the rift, it caused you to meet him. Only then did you get sent through time. You are a paradox."

"Yeah. I've been called that before, actually. Now get out of the doorway and let me through."

"Not until I get my son back!"

Ryder tried to force his way through the stranger, but his thirteen-year-old body was not strong enough to get past the full-grown man. Eddie shoved back at the boy with all his might, and he pushed the boy backward across the room until they were at the windowed side of the room.

Already running backward just to keep his balance, Duncan collided with the radiator next to the wall. His body went limp again, but the elder Ryder's soul remained.

In pain and fury, he yelled, "I can't feel my legs! You bastard! Look what you've done!"

"Where is my son?" the stranger yelled with hot anger.

A man the children would recognize as Principal Stockton, if they were awake, arrived in the doorway. He had heard shouting from Woods's history class from down the hall. Assuming there was a disciplinary problem, he figured he may be needed and rushed to Woods's aid.

A man stood on the far side of the room, a man who was screaming for his son.

"Excuse me, sir. I'm Principal Stockton. How can I help you?"

The man turned to face him but gave no answer nor introduction. Instead, he shrieked and clasped his hands over his ears.

Eddie fell to his knees, resisting the devil possession Ryder was attempting.

With the stranger now on his knees, Principal Stockton caught a glimpse of the limp body of Duncan Ryder slumped on the floor.

The stranger was cringing in pain and thrust his hands in front of himself to prevent falling on his face. Blood ran down his cheek and dripped on the ugly orange carpet.

Mr. Woods seemed to be asleep; he and his class all sat at their desks, their heads resting on their arms as though napping. Principal Stockton turned to run back to his office and call 911.

As he ran down the hall, Eddie with Ryder inside his brain screamed out the word "Bastard!"

Stockton turned to face the man, who was now writhing on the floor as though in an epileptic seizure. Stockton turned again and ran toward his office.

The Eddie and Duncan together in Eddie's body grasped the leg of Ryder's nearby empty desk. He pulled himself up from the floor and then turned the desk upside down. Now its legs were in the air like the struggling beetle's legs had been.

As if to squash the desk like the beetle, the man stomped his foot down on the bottom of the desk. With a tremendous show of strength that no one else could see, he wrenched one of the metal legs from the desk, bending it first one way and then the next and back until he ripped it right off.

He held the sharp end over the boy's limp body like a spear. It was pointed at Duncan's heart. Was it sharp enough to pierce the child's heart?

He then grasped the piece of bluish-gray leg as if it were a baseball bat. He raised it to crush the boy's skull with a mighty swing.

"Stop!" Woods cried out. "Are you crazy?"

Unable to take full control of Eddie, Ryder had left and reentered Woods. He sent his chair crashing to the floor and staggered away from the desk. His feet were numb, and he fell to the floor so he dragged his body toward the assailant with his hands.

Eddie was on his knees now, raising the weapon like a golf club. He swung.

His empty fists whooshed past the boy's face. He had swung with empty hands, and the weight of the swing took him off balance and he fell to the floor. He rolled over on the ugly carpet to see Stockton standing above him with the desk leg in his hand and eyes wide.

"Principal Stockton. Thank you." The weary voice came from the boy, and now Woods's body lay limp on the carpet beside his desk. Ryder had taken the easiest form he could, his younger self.

Now the boy turned to Eddie. "I'm disappointed. It's supposed to be a wooden stake through the heart. That's made of metal."

"I was fresh out of silver bullets, wooden stakes, and holy water."

Eddie felt a wetness on his cheek. He wiped his hand across it. Yep. It was blood from his ear.

"Where is my son?" he asked.

"In time," the boy replied.

What is that smell? Stockton thought. A gas leak! So that was what has caused this insanity.

He himself had felt a terrible headache and then a sensation that he was not in control of his own body. He was not sure how he managed to disarm the man in front of him.

Now Stockton shook a nearby student awake. He didn't expect it to work, but the child raised his head. He looked around. How could he possibly wake each child?

But as he looked across the room, student heads were popping up all over.

"Children!" he cried. "I want you all to go out to the flagpole and wait for me there." He put a hand on the shoulder of the boy he'd awakened. "And, Mr. Desoto, pull the fire alarm on your way out."

Woods now scrambled to his feet again; this time he could feel the floor beneath him. "Follow me, children," he said and led the way.

Without fear, but with s weak and timid-sounding voice, Duncan spoke. "I'm going to die."

"No, you won't," Stockton assured him. "We'll get you to a hospital."

"I was talking to Eddie."

Just then the alarm sounded.

"Single file, children," Stockton said as though he had always been minding his own business.

"Tell me where my son is before you die," Eddie groaned.

"Jesus! You still don't get it. He's not your son, Eddie."

"And how do you suddenly know my name?"

"I always knew God was an idiot." Ryder sighed.

Eddie paused. He realized suddenly that this was not the same Ryder whom he had met earlier. Now it was the Ryder who had written him the ransom note.

"You already left and came back, didn't you?"

"That's good. Now put the rest together," the devil in Duncan said. "Why are you the master of the rift? How can you move in and out of the rift without the Christiansen platform?"

"What is the Christiansen platform?"

"That little round surface that was there when Dr. Maris pulled you through the rift."

"I don't know how, the rift just appeared and I assumed they finally found out how to bring us back. We went through and came out in a room with what looked like space suits on the wall."

"And then what?'

"We put them on. And the rift opened up again. So we went through. Wait. Was that you who hit my nose when putting the helmet on my suit?"

"It was me and the King."

"You keep talking about gods and kings and such. I have no idea what you mean."

"You're never gonna get there, are you?"

"I don't think I like these games."

"Why did you try to kill me a minute ago?"

"If I killed you now, you would never be able to take my son to begin with."

"I told you, he's not your son. Well, he is and he isn't."

"Why are you so cryptic? Just tell me what the hell you're talking about."

"Eddie, Maris is not your father. He never was."

"Are you saying . . . ?"

"Yes, Eddie. You fathered yourself, you idiot!"

"In San Francisco?"

"Now you're catching on."

"But that's not possible." Eddie really was an idiot back then.

"And time travel is?"

"Well, of course. We have both done it."

"Cause and effect, Eddie. You are fucking around with cause and effect. You are still living with linear time as a model in your brain. You said yourself that cause can proceed the effect. Remember?"

Eddie was silent. Taking it in.

"You're immortal, Eddie. And not like 'the Highlander.' You could cut your head off and still live on although not in the same way."

"Let's assume I won't try that, ever."

"Did you also take the desk leg out of my hand?" he asked.

"Sort of. Ever hear someone say 'the devil made me do it'?"

"Only the devil possesses people."

"Is that so? Then I guess Woods was right." He laughed.

"So then you are?"

"If you are the Father and the Son, why can't I be the Holy Spirit? Why do you assume I have to be the devil?"

"You are what you are."

"Remember, you said that."

"Why?"

"Because you are the Great I am."

"You're still talking nonsense. Did you take my son or not?"

"I took you, Eddie. Can't you feel it? Don't you somehow know what I did?"

Just then, Stockton ran in. "An ambulance is on the way, Duncan. Don't you worry." He looked at the now-seated Eddie, assessing the possible threat.

"I'm fine, Mr. Stockton. This is my uncle Eddie. Everything is all right. Just as it should be."

"But he—"

"No, he wasn't really going to hurt me. It was a mistake."

"Maybe the gas was making him hallucinate?" Stockton offered.

"Perhaps. But he's fine now. There's no more gas."

In the distance, the premature lawn mower had gone silent and was replaced now with the sound of a siren. Stockton rushed out so he could usher the firemen and the paramedics into the room.

***

This is how the Almighty God, doing business as a young woman named Denise Thomson, became the mother of the Almighty God in human form.

When Eddie realized Guinness was not coming to the alley in Chinatown to rescue them, he led Maris out of the alley, and they began walking. He listened to Maris for almost an hour before telling him where they were going.

From Chinatown, they made their way to Haight-Ashbury where the Diggers would offer them food for free. Eddie knew this because his father had told him stories about the Diggers when he was just a boy.

Maris had brought through the little platform from the return room with him to 1967. They could, in theory, use it again to enter the rift and return safely to the future. But if they traveled to the future with it, they would leave behind an active portal in 1967.

Eddie decided he needed to find a way to open the portal and still take the device with them to the future.

Eddie had read a lot of books, but seen very few movies in his lifetime. He did once go to watch *Back to the Future* with Dr. Maris. He had told the young Eddie that he himself had a way to travel through time if only he could find the missing piece, which he likened to the flux capacitor in *Back to the Future*.

He found his flux capacitor when Guinness stole the Christiansen Project.

Eddie's plan was formed from his memory of that movie. He would take the Christiansen Project to its original inventor to modify it so they could take it with them through the rift. And at that time, the inventor was less than five miles away at San Francisco State College's physics department.

As soon as they were on their feet, so to speak, he would take the flawed return device to Christiansen to adapt it to his needs.

Denise met the odd pair in Haight-Ashbury. They were selling grilled cheese sandwiches to hungry hippies for a dime apiece. The older one, Henry, grilled them on a camp stove, and the younger, Eddie, collected dimes.

Eddie got the idea from people who followed the Grateful Dead on tour. Some people, his father had told him when he was young, funded their trips around the nation in this way.

In the Summer of Love, when Denise bought her first grilled cheese sandwich, the Marises could bring in as much as two and a half dollars an hour, a dime at a time. With the Diggers giving food out for free nearby, one would not expect them to thrive charging for their sandwiches. But thrive they did.

They found a nearby apartment they could rent, and every night, Eddie would plug in the device and open the portal so that Guinness could come through to rescue them. As spring turned to summer, however, he began to realize they were on their own to find a way back.

The younger Dr. Christiansen was then teaching at San Francisco State College (later known as San Francisco State University). He had not yet even conceived of the project, however, and when he reverse engineered the small platform device and developed a battery-operated version for Eddie, he left San Francisco for Stanford and began developing his own prototype.

For reasons unknown to anyone at that time, the move to Stanford caused Tylee Christiansen to be born a boy, and he was named Tyler.

In this new history, Tyler never had Tylee's accident, and when he met Duncan Ryder, he was a new nurse at Cheney Home and Duncan was a resident there, confined to a wheelchair.

When Tylee's being born a boy came to the attention of the devil, Ryder in his future form, he could have corrected her birth to make her a she once again, and he planned to do so. He had the power at his disposal to fix the circumstance by transferring a girl embryo into her mother instead of the boy embryo.

This process was also how when Denise Thompson became the mother of the Son of God, that Elvis himself would be the one to transfer that embryo to a virgin named Mary. Well, Duncan Ryder, using Elvis as his puppet, anyway.

Ryder came out of the rift in the body of Elvis to impregnate Tylee's mother with an embryo that would become a girl rather than a boy.

But then he remembered that she had wrecked her car in 1996, and as a boy, Tyler did not suffer that fate. In this new reality, Ryder was crippled in the seventh grade by Eddie.

Tyler was uninjured and became a nurse. The two came into contact again at Cheney home, their roles reversed. When he saw all this, the young devil left him a him.

***

The Almighty God in the physical form of Principal Stockton opened the front door of the schoolhouse as the last of the children, except for Ryder, lined up at the flagpole and the emergency responders rushed in.

First firemen then paramedics were rushing into the classroom now.

"I really am dumbfounded that you still don't comprehend your own destiny, your identity," Ryder said through the lips of his younger self.

"Soon, Eddie," he went on, "you will see me die. I know because I have seen it through your eyes already."

"When? Where?"

"Forget that for now, Eddie. I know my destiny. I now know my place. My identity. Yours is yet to be written, in your mind at least."

"Duncan?"

"Yes?" He was being strapped to a backboard.

"What is your destiny, your place, and identity?"

Duncan laughed. "Death is my destiny. Your enemy is my place. And . . ." He sang the next part: "Pleased to meet you. Hope you guess my name."

"Satan?"

"I'm your enemy. Your ultimate evil that allows your incompetent, bumbling immortality to become the definition of ultimate good. I am death, you are life. I am darkness, you are the light of the world."

"Ultimate good?"

"Yes, my Creator." He would have bowed were he not immobilized and at that moment being hoisted into the air and strapped to a rolling bed.

Eddie scrambled along beside the rolling bed; apparently the paramedics assumed he was family.

"Do you even realize where I have been the last few minutes?" Ryder asked.

"You were right here. You entered my mind, but you fled back to this broken body, which apparently nearly killed you."

"When you were pulling the leg off that desk, where do suppose I was then?"

"I don't know. Time traveling, I suppose."

"Yes. I have lived thousands of years in thousands of times while you were preparing to kill me."

"Lived through others? Without your body, I mean."

"Mostly. Yes. I was trying to outwit you, to kill you, to take your place, or at least cocreate all this."

"But you couldn't kill me?"

"No, Eddie. That is my parting curse to you. I will go to the grave and face possible nothingness or the birth of something new. But you are doomed to the 'gift' of everlasting life. A continued existence. It's the one thing I can have that you cannot. You will never feel death's sting."

A hand grasped Eddie's elbow, and the paramedic guided him into the back of the ambulance. When Eddie looked at him, he saw a trail of dried blood down his cheek that seemed to have come from the man's ear.

"Yes," the youth smiled on the stretcher. "I've traveled to this time as well."

"Good to see you again, Master." The other paramedic smiled from the open door of the ambulance. No blood was coming from his ears, but Eddie knew the face well.

"Dad!" Eddie shouted.

But Maris, dressed as a paramedic, replied, "Nope. Call me Lucifer." And he closed the door.

"You've seen two Marises at the same place and time, but you can't accept three of me?" the patient said to the astonished young God.

"That isn't you!" Eddie protested. "It's my dad, Dr. Henry Maris."

Maris stepped into the passenger seat and turned to face Eddie. "This body is a favorite of mine. I damaged it once, you know."

Maris pointed to his forehead. "There was a ton of information up here, and when I forced it out of him, he didn't heal up like you or me. Kind of like a mind rape that left him scarred for life. He may be a time traveler like us, but he's not like us, Eddie. He's a mortal. A very intelligent mortal."

Though the ambulance roared and whined its way down the street, it would never reach a hospital.

"You'll get him back, kid. Don't worry," the Lucifer inside Maris said as he turned and put on his seatbelt. "I've used him to travel. You understand?"

"No, I don't."

"Like Billy Pilgrim," the immobile patient explained. "I came unstuck in time. You know that reference, right?"

Eddie nodded. He had to read Vonnegut's *Slaughterhouse 5* in an English class before he dropped out of college.

Ryder continued. "But I only came in essence, spirit, consciousness. I have no body. I'm a naked soul, lost in time."

"This is why"—the driver spoke for the first time—"you felt such pain when I forced my way into your 'shell,' and it's why some ears bleed." He pointed to drips of blood on his cheek.

"I can only move about and affect the world in linear time if I am in a body," he continued.

"Like Sam Beckett," Lucifer said.

"Until you broke it," the patient added. "This was the most pain-free body I ever was in. Now look at me! Maybe I could be another Stephen Hawking, but fuck theories, I wanted to experience time in a body that works."

"So," said Lucifer from the passenger seat, "I use this body a lot. I can travel from place to place and time to time without hurting anyone else with a possession. There's no need to force my way in."

"Well, sometimes it's necessary. But this guy's okay. It may look like an aneurism, but a little dab with a cotton swab, and he'll be fine."

Eddie turned to Maris's shell and asked, "I don't get it. Sam Beckett? The playwright?"

"Oh wait," said the patient. "Déjà vu."

The driver and Lucifer laughed in unison. Eddie felt sure the joke was on him.

"Remember that picture," Maris's puppet master asked, "that picture Enid taped on her notebook at the Provo Project, where she drew a lip print on the guy's cheek?"

"The TV guy?"

"Yeah, the TV guy. That Sam Beckett. He jumped into bodies of strangers from the past and lived a piece of their life for them. It was called *Quantum Leap.*"

Right then, Eddie realized that the siren on the ambulance had been turned off long ago. The ambulance was on a gravel road, and all Eddie could see out the windshield was trees. The driver stopped and turned around in his seat.

"Well, here we are," he said.

"Here we are," Lucifer echoed.

His eyes darted from face to face in obvious distress. He had been riding in the back swallowing the two men and the teen's story without question. And one of them had identified himself as the Father of Lies, Lucifer. Now he doubted everything he had heard, especially the part about him being immortal. He was very frightened now.

Eddie reached into his coat pocket and pulled out the Christiansen Project.

Before he could activate it, faster than he could follow, Lucifer snatched it away from him.

"You said you didn't even know what that was. And here you sit with the damned thing in your pocket all along."

Eddie had pulled a Colonel Guinness move. He and his "father" had stolen the device from Christiansen in San Francisco.

Undeterred, Eddie raised a fist above the nose of the immobile youth. "No one move, or his nose goes in so far he will smell his cerebellum."

"Really, Eddie?" Lucifer chided. "You're going to kill a thirteen-year-old boy who's already on his deathbed?"

"Hm," the boy mused. "We have a standoff, do we?"

The pain instantly raced through Eddie's brain. It felt like something had pierced his own brain all the way to the cerebellum. He'd felt the boy inside his head before, and he knew what was happening now.

Through blinding pain, he carried out his threat and drove the boy's septum into his brain, killing him quickly. Before he even opened his eyes, Eddie's pain was gone.

Even as blood spurted out, the boy's lips were moving. But the voice did not issue from his lips. Instead, the voice echoed from all around the ambulance walls like the voice of a choir of all baritones.

"Ouch!" the voice rang.

Lucifer laughed. The stunned driver looked at Eddie. "Look what you've done," he said. "You got blood all over this pretty ambulance."

"You know," Lucifer said through Maris, "he came here to die. We were here to help him, but now you've done the job for us."

"It didn't work," the driver said.

"No, no." Lucifer grinned. "Not yet."

He pointed the little round device at Eddie as if it were a gun. He seemed ready to shift the traveler's atoms. *What is he waiting for?* Eddie wondered.

Maris's puppet master was grinning like a Cheshire cat. "What was God's greatest trick, Eddie?"

He had heard that he was God Almighty a lot lately. Not reassured that he was actually immortal, Eddie did not say, "Raising the dead." If he had, he surmised, the villain would shoot him. It could be used to kill. Eddie knew this. He tried to change the topic.

"Trick? Don't you mean his greatest miracle?"

"All right, my squirming friend, what was God's greatest miracle?"

Eddie stalled.

"Come on. It's not a trick question. What miracle stands out? What proves that God is God?"

"The creation of heaven and Earth?"

"No one saw him actually do that, so we can't prove or disprove it."

"Ah, good point. The answer then is his vanishing act."

"His what?"

"Well, he creates the universe then disappears somewhere beyond the quasars. And he's never heard from again."

"That sounds like the voice of an atheist." Lucifer laughed. "But a good point. Just like Frankenstein cast out his monster. And now we've gone to find the Creator so we can destroy him for this horrible injustice."

"He offers eternal life, and we say, 'Why did you give us life to begin with?' What a horrible gift!"

"He is playing God again." Lucifer laughed.

"Yes." Eddie actually laughed in agreement.

Maris's hand raised his weapon again. "Try again, Eddie. Greatest miracle?"

"That's not it?"

"No. Greatest trick maybe, but you amended the question yourself. Remember? Greatest MIRACLE, come on now."

"Uh okay. How about the miracle of the eight-fold path?"

"Wrong culture. Wrong religion. You're a Protestant, and we both know it. Leave Buddha out of this."

"Oh yes. My religion is in my file back at the CIA, isn't it?"

"Come on. Quit stalling. Trickery is the devil's bag, and you just don't have it in you."

"I DON'T have it in me!"

"You still can answer my question."

"I sure hope so. I get the feeling if I don't get it right, you're going to kill me."

"Oh, I may either way, but not yet." His previous grin was gone now. He believed he was playing guessing games with an idiot. He decided it was time to drop hints.

"What was Jesus's greatest miracle to prove his divinity?"

"Actually, I'm a Unitarian," Eddie said even though all of them knew he was Lutheran.

"What?"

"Unitarian."

"Don't believe the divinity of Jesus?"

"Right."

"If you were really a Unitarian, you would have a better idea what they believe in now instead of what they believed in the 1500s."

"I told you I don't believe in the divinity of Jesus."

"You are Lutheran, and you're familiar with the Christian interpretations. Even if you converted to Unitarianism, you can still answer the question."

"Oh, I know! Walking on water!"

"Later," the devil coached.

Eddie looked at the driver again as though he would help with an answer. The driver had seemed to be watching a tennis tournament, his eyes darting back and forth, waiting for his companion to score game point.

"Later?" Eddie said. "The crucifixion? Salvation, the forgiveness of sin?"

"Goddamn it, Eddie! The crucifixion is the devil's finest hour! That's the moment the monster strangles Frankenstein's bride. The revenge against the master! What FOLLOWED the death that proved Jesus was the Christ, goddamn it?"

"Um, the, uh—"

"Don't you dare say the ascension, Eddie! It's what we celebrate on Easter Sunday. They even have Easter in the Unitarian churches."

He could not play the fool any longer, and Eddie considered bolting out the back door. He'd never make it. *Oh, what the hell!* he thought.

"You mean the resurrection?"

"The resurrection!" he cried. He was genuinely happy the guessing game was done.

"And now, ladies and gentlemen," Lucifer began his show, "you'll notice there is nothing up my sleeve . . . I wave my magic . . . what the hell is this thing called anyway?"

"The Christiansen Project." The prisoner sighed. "But before you wave it and make me disappear, can you at least tell me who you really are?"

"I told you, Eddie. I am the devil, the angel of light, Beelzebub, Mephistopheles, the dark prince, Satan, Feklar, for Christ's sake!"

"Feklar? I never heard that one before."

"Sorry. That's another television reference. You know what your problem is, Eddie?"

"Yeah. I put my trust in a man I thought was my dad. And now I find out that he's an agent for the wrong team, who claims to be possessed by the devil. And he's about to scatter my molecules around the back of an ambulance. Is that the problem you were thinking of?"

"No. You're a literary snob."

"What?"

"He's right," the driver finally spoke. "You know who Billy Pilgrim is. You know who the wrong Sam Beckett is. But if we mention *Quantum Leap*, *Doctor Who*, or *Star Trek*, you are a deer in the headlights. You probably never even owned a television set."

"At least I'm not living in a fantasy world."

"Oh, don't piss me off, Eddie," Lucifer scolded. He looked at the driver. "Ready?"

"Ready."

"Wait, goddamn it!" Eddie pleaded.

"What's this, Eddie? Pleading for your life? I told you I can't kill you. That trick is not in the show."

"Let's do it already," the driver added.

"Okay."

Eddie braced himself to have his molecules scattered. Instead, the devil fired and Eddie was in the rift, a warm and comfortable place.

When he came back into the world, his eyes were still closed but nonetheless burning from the citrus in the rift.

He was still in the ambulance when he opened his eyes, but the blood was gone and the dead boy was sitting up on the cot and smiling.

"Ta-da!" cried the paramedics in unison.

"The resurrection!" Ryder cried.

Both paramedics got out, singing "Hallelujah!" They walked to the back of the ambulance, and the back door swung open.

"Thank you. Thank you," Ryder said, bowing at the waist. "It's good to be back. But something about that really pissed me off. Somebody break his fucking nose."

"My pleasure!" said the driver as his fist swiftly flew at Eddie's face.

***

This is how the Almighty God doing business as Eddie Maris, in the Summer of Love, fathered the Son of God.

"It's the Fourth of July," Denise said, grabbing Eddie's hand and pulling him toward the door. "I want to go out and have some fun. Come on!"

Eddie, having worked so hard to earn a meager living selling sandwiches, had not even known it was July the Fourth. But he was ready to cut loose and have a little fun so he let himself be led out of the apartment and into the street.

Eddie and Denise stepped onto the sidewalk, and immediately, they jumped at the gunshot-like popping of firecrackers at their feet.

"Sorry!" Dr. Maris yelled to his time-traveling companion. "I just lighted them and I didn't see you."

"Be careful! You could have hurt us!" Eddie screamed back over the racket. "Those things are dangerous!"

"You's safe," Maris said. "I only had the one package."

"So you're done with them, right?"

"All done." Maris smiled.

"He's fine," Denise insisted. "Let's go have some fun tonight."

"Okay," Eddie agreed. "I guess I could use a fun night out."

"You want a fun night out?" a voice said. It was a neighbor named Seth. Seth Andrews lived in the apartment next door, and he had met them at their grilled cheese stand, the second day they set it up.

"I can help you out with that," Seth continued. He pulled out a little plastic bag with four sugar cubes inside. He pulled one out and popped it in his mouth. "Hold out your hands," he commanded.

Denise smiled and held her hand out as commanded. Seth gave her one of the sugar cubes, and she too popped it in her mouth.

"Just suck on it," Seth said. "Don't chew it. Just let it dissolve on your tongue.

"Here, Ed. Take one," he offered.

"Sugar? What's so fun about that?"

"Trust me. You'll have the time of your life."

Henry held out his hand and accepted one of the cubes as well.

"Come on," he said. "You wanted to have some fun tonight. So have a little."

"One left." Seth smiled. "It's got your name on it, Eddie. I promise you will see fireworks tonight even if you stay inside."

Eddie relented and accepted the sugar cube that he was destined to take on this summer evening.

Of course, the cubes were more than just sugar, and soon all four of them were seeing the fireworks Seth had promised.

The Almighty God believing himself to be a young hippie named Seth had only come to the door because he had heard the firecrackers going off when he was about to take some LSD he'd recently scored. They were acid-laced sugar cubes, a popular way to take acid.

Eddie honestly did not think to ask if the sugar was laced with acid, which would seem odd with all the things Maris had told him about the Summer of Love.

The shrieks and bangs of neighborhood fireworks seemed louder and closer to Eddie than they really were. Every sound repeated in an echo inside his head. Every flash of light also seemed to repeat in a sort of visual echo. His feet seemed to sink into the street as he walked, being led by Denise, who held his hand.

Their hands were joined. Eddie felt that his soul was also joined with Denise. He felt a connection to her that was more than hand-to-hand contact. It was as though they were joined like two neighboring puzzle pieces. Their hands and their souls were made to fit together perfectly.

He only half realized that Denise had led him around the block and back inside the apartment. Seth and Maris had walked on somewhere. They would be gone all night. Somehow, Eddie knew that they would be gone all night.

He felt home. Like he was where he belonged rather than a man stranded in the past. When Denise kissed him and sat him down on the sofa he had slept on the night before, it felt like he was right where he needed to be. He was destined to be here with her at this moment.

He leaned in and kissed her back and again saw fireworks. He'd known Denise for less than a month, but he knew now she was his soul mate. The love of his life and the most beautiful woman on the planet. And now her hand was undoing his belt. Or was it his own hand? He wasn't sure. But it was her hand. His hand was pulling on her shirt, and the other hand was reaching inside it.

He was aroused like never before. Even more than when he lost his virginity to an older woman, the neighbor lady. She was tender, loving, and beautiful. But even she did not compare to this electric moment.

For her part, Denise had never been so turned on as she was at this moment either. This was not her first rodeo, nor her first acid trip. But his was the most beautiful body she'd ever undressed.

It was the first time she ever felt totally in love. She felt like Eddie was someone she had known her whole life. She had known him, loved him, forever. Throughout all time, she had known and loved him, and this was the first time she ever said it and showed it.

When the moment came, it came for both of them. Their shared orgasm was the most intense and simply awesome orgasm for the both of them. No experience would or could ever compare to this moment of pure ecstasy.

They did not know it yet, but they had created a child that night. And certainly neither of them had any idea that the two of them were Eddie's own parents.

***

This is how the Almighty God, believing himself to be the freed soul of Duncan Ryder, transitioned from God in human form to devil in spirit form.

Ryder had discovered Eddie's bungled transformation to an immortal, and he wanted to gain the immortality Eddie had.

He wanted to travel through time as Eddie did in his own body. Eddie had created a whopper of a paradox in becoming his own father.

If he could only bring his adult body through the rift, he could do the same. But he had left that body in stasis in the future, and now Duncan's future body was crippled by Eddie in that seventh-grade classroom.

He tried inhabiting his own body the day before the crippling. He tried to seduce his mother in the past. But there was no way his mother was going to go for a thirteen-year-old boy.

He then collected his own sperm and in the form of Elvis collected an egg from his sleeping mother and grew an embryo in a petri dish to implant into his mother's womb.

On the night Ryder's father and mother were about to conceive Duncan, the devil entered the room in spirit and in the body of the King.

This was his first time in one place and time in two separate forms. Ryder possessed his father. Instead of waking and seducing Duncan's mother, as Duncan's puppet, Mr. Ryder went to the bathroom and quietly masturbated instead.

While he was gone, Elvis carefully removed the woman's egg from her uterus. Later, by Ryder's perception, that egg would be fertilized with Duncan's sperm and grown into an embryo in a petri dish.

Then Elvis implanted the fertilized egg into the womb of Mrs. Ryder. In this way, Duncan succeeded in becoming his own father, and he was now an immortal.

Soon, Ryder set out to become the one true God. The only way to do that was to kill the bungling time traveler that was Eddie.

Then he began to try killing Eddie before he could ever travel through time in the first place. Yet after every kill, Ryder would return to the rift, and there was the Eddie being dragged into the rift for the first time by Dr. Maris, the man he believed was his father.

Once in the rift, always in the rift, he decided after trying time and time again.

He could never undo Eddie. He was self-created and could not be uncreated by the young devil. He was the "I am."

Finally, Ryder realized it was a matter of destiny; he was not destined to be the only physically immortal soul. Instead, he was destined to become Eddie's enemy.

Eventually, it occurred to him that Eddie had fathered himself and then been dragged through the rift the very first time in the original history.

If that had not happened, Ryder would never have been under the mountain in Utah to begin with. And he would never leave his body early and become an immortal time-traveling spirit.

He himself had been created by the original actions of Eddie the first time he ever entered the rift. If Eddie did not enter the rift and father himself, he would never be, so Ryder would never be immortal, would never travel through time and space as a free soul. That is why, he reasoned, that he could never kill Eddie.

But which came first? The Father or the Son? Did God create man before man created God?

This became his new plan. If Eddie was now a god, Duncan would use him to create the one true God. Eddie, who had been dragged into the rift by another man and foolishly fathered himself, would become the great creator. He would be the Father and the Son.

He devised a plan to create life using Eddie's DNA. Thereby, Eddie would truly be God. He would be the creation and the creator. He would be truly God in the flesh.

***

This is how the Almighty God in the form of a custodian named Eddie Maris became the Creator of life on earth.

Everyone knows life began in the water. But primordial ooze or underwater volcanic vents? Or a combination of both? Well, it was actually in a geothermic hot pool of water.

"Are we finally saved?" Eddie asked his father as they came out of the rift into a room with no one else in it.

Two suits hung on the wall. They looked like space suits to Eddie.

"What is this? Some kind of decontamination room?" Eddie asked, knowing his dull-witted father would not know the answer.

But he did. He smiled. "Eddie, it's me again," he said. "I know what I'm doing now. And I know what we are here for."

"Dad?" Eddie paused. "Okay. I guess if you know what to do, tell me."

"We have to put on these suits."

While they dressed, Dr. Maris explained that they were going to complete a mission to fix the timeline. "We damaged things, you see. But first we have to get some important information."

The suits were more complicated and more uncomfortable than Eddie expected. They needed one another's help to secure the helmets and to adjust the flow of oxygen.

"Ow! Damn it!" Eddie yelled as the helmet in his father's hands hit him in the nose.

"Sorry."

"That really hurt! Oh crap, Dad, I'm bleeding!"

Maris had already snatched a first aid kit from the wall nearby. He pulled out and opened some thick gauze and held it to Eddie's nosebleed. In a matter of a few minutes, they had stopped the flow of blood, and Maris carefully attached Eddie's helmet.

In a matter of time that seemed like hours, they were finally dressed and ready to find out how life began on earth.

When they were both dressed and ready, they picked up some instruments and headed back into the rift. "I know just where to go. Don't worry," Maris said.

During this trip through the rift, they smelled no trace of citrus, and their eyes did not burn. Their helmets filtered out its sting.

They came out right at the edge of a boiling pool of water with sharp rocks all around. Maris had explained to his son that the scientists looked through the rift and they believed this was the very pool of boiling water in which life first formed on Earth. It was the primordial soup.

The pair was here, Maris said, to take a sample of the water back to the lab to study. The scientists wanted to know what molecules were first to evolve into life-forms.

Eddie was leaning out over the pool with what he was told was a collection container when his father brushed by with his own collection container. Why they needed two samples was beyond comprehension to Eddie.

Eddie's visor was clouded with steam, but he could still see Maris reaching past him. Instead of dipping his container like he told Eddie to do, he dumped something into the pool. It disappeared too fast for Eddie to follow, but he did see something red and white.

The red and white thing was actually the bloody gauze Maris had used on Eddie's nose. According to plan, Eddie's DNA thus formed the first building blocks of life.

Already, you know Maris was not himself when he did this. He was possessed. And as Eddie would say about four and a half billion years later, "only the devil possesses people."

***

The Almighty God in the form of a young carpenter named Joseph saw a white-skinned man appear out of nothingness. The man was wearing a white suit with sparkling jewels all over it. The chest of the suit bore a gold likeness of a lightning bolt with letters you would recognize at "TCB" on it. Joseph could not read the letters. The strange man looked like no one Joseph had ever seen.

He told Joseph not to be afraid. He told him his bride-to-be would bear a child even though she had never known a man.

Joseph saw that the angel held a strange and beautiful object. It was smoother than any sanded wood. It was round and white. It was made primarily of plastic, something completely alien to the mortal man.

When he'd delivered his message, the angel pointed the flat surface of the object at his belly, and quickly a cloud began to encircle him and he faded from view. A strange cloud remained that Joseph could smell but not identify. A sweet but tangy odor that he guessed was a sign his visitor was divine.

On the same night, his bride, Mary, was awakened by a strange rumbling sensation in her belly. The same angel, they concluded, had visited them both that night.

Mary saw the same smooth white object in the angel's hands, but it was pointed at her belly rather than the angel's.

He told her she would bear a child in nine months' time. He told her not to fear. He told her what to name the child.

But this part of the Savior's story you already know, don't you?

Duncan Ryder, traveling through time in the form of only his soul, found he could travel in the body of others. And Elvis had become one of his favorite bodies in which to travel.

Close to his death and full of drugs, Elvis had been an easy person to possess. At first, he traveled within Elvis in blue pajamas, but he returned to the house at different times to change his wardrobe. He liked to travel in Elvis dressed in his finest concert clothing.

His travels led to sightings of "the King" in all sorts of places and times and to rumors that Elvis was working for the CIA and that his death had been faked.

The Almighty God, believing himself to be a boy named Eddie Maris, was born on April 4, 1968, just a few moments after another man called "King" died in Memphis, Tennessee. He was also born some 1968 years earlier in a place called the City of David, there believing himself the son of a carpenter named Joseph. Years later, he would be known as Jesus of Nazareth.

***

When the Almighty God as Eddie Maris awoke, he was unsure how much time had passed since his nose was broken in the back of the ambulance.

Now he saw Maris's face above him. He was sitting in a slouched position on a sofa. He could not feel his hands, his arms, his legs.

He lifted his hands to his face. He could see them, but they seemed to belong to someone else.

"No, no, no!" Maris said, pulling Eddie's hands away from his face. "Don't touch the bandages. Your nose is broken so bad we had to let Jerry the paramedic out to play."

"¿Quien es Jerry?" a voice like Eddie's, only like he was holding his nose shut, inquired.

"Jerry is the paramedic who drove you here. He reset your nose and loaded you up with drugs."

"My whole life," said Jerry the paramedic, "I never would have guessed I would one day break God's nose. And then reset it."

"Exciting, isn't it?" Maris smiled. He was clearly still Lucifer. "Oh yes, Eddie, Jerry is under my control again."

"¿Mi naríz está rota?" Eddie asked.

"Yes. Eddie, your nose is broken," Jerry said. "Why is he speaking in Spanish?"

"Good question. Why are you speaking in Spanish, Eduardo?"

"¡No hablo Español!" Eddie insisted, and suddenly realized he was doing just that. He had no idea why or how, but he was now fluent in Spanish.

"He must have crossed purposes with another version of himself in the rift," the Maris puppet offered. "With his inexperience level, that would disorient him. Do you think you're in Mexico, Eduardo?"

"I . . . I don't know Spanish," Eddie replied haltingly as though English were a new language to him.

"Well, you do now, don't you, Eduardo?"

"It's time," Ryder said. Only now did Eddie realize he was in the room as well.

"Time for what?" Eddie asked.

"Time for me to give you my parting gift, Ed."

"Gift? What gift? What are you talking about?" His mouth was dry from using it to breathe and was just starting to feel again. The numbness was abating, and his nose throbbed.

"I told you I was going to die. But it's not enough to win the race to the grave. I'm going to give you a parting gift. The all-at-once," the boy said. "I'm leaving you with the eternal now. Then I will die."

"What is that?"

"What is it not?" Duncan answered cryptically.

"It's the sum of his perception," Lucifer as Maris said. "All of his memories in a quick dump."

"You know," Duncan said, "when I entered your mind— how long ago was it for you? About an hour ago? When our thoughts and our spirits collided, you fought with me, but I forced my way in and stole your thoughts from you.

"But you learned from me too. Didn't you, Eddie?"

"I guess so."

"Of course you did. But you know what? You are the only one who ever learned anything from me, and you're the only one who could ever keep secrets from me."

Lucifer spoke up now: "You are going to see and learn and feel and know everything I know. More, in fact. You will know everything HE knows."

"Everything," echoed the broken body of the boy.

"You will know his thoughts," Lucifer continued, "his fears and anxieties, his loves, envies, and jealousies. You get it all."

Eddie looked over to the boy. "Your last will and testament?"

"Something like that."

"What if I refuse?"

"Dr. Maris refused. You saw what happened to him."

Eddie wiggled his fingers. He could feel them again. They were separate, individual digits again, no longer was his hand a numb lump of flesh.

His nose, however, felt frozen to his face, and he was aware that his voice was altered. His sinuses were blocked up, packed with damp gauze. He could breathe only through his cotton-dry mouth.

His lips felt tacky as though he had just been kissing a ball of tape. He licked them with a dry tongue, rough like a cat's.

"So I have to submit to some kind of mental merge, some kind of brainwashing, or be totally lobotomized. Is that it?" He licked his lips again; then he wiped them on the back of his hand, which stretched a thread of blood and spit between his lips and hand. It was a thread that would not break until it was nearly two feet long. He could see the bloody saliva smeared on the back of his hand.

"Brainwashing?" Lucifer mocked. "No, Eddie. It's more like a spiritual and mental lovemaking."

"A great fuck," the boy said.

"Oh? A mind fuck, you say?"

"Funny, Eddie," the voice of Maris said. "But we're just playing with you, Ed. You won't get hurt by this. Not one drop of blood will come from your ears like you saw happen to others."

"You see, Ed," the boy continued, "I could rip you open like a cantaloupe and never spill a drop. I can storm the walls of your mental defenses and know you more intimately than you know yourself. Hell, man, I already do. I know all your secrets."

"But that is not what this is about," Lucifer added.

"No, Ed. This is about me giving myself to you. All of me." The boy coughed. A trickle of blood ran from the corner of his mouth and down his chin.

"How much time do we have?" young Ryder asked. "It can't be long now."

"Just a couple more minutes," Jerry the paramedic said, glancing at his watch.

"Then let's get on with this before Jonah gets here. I need to gloat when I die."

Lucifer laughed.

Eddie coughed and gagged on some bloody mucous in his throat. That made him feel as though he was punched in the nose all over again. His whole head throbbed painfully with every beat of his heart.

"Eddie," Duncan soothed, "get comfortable, sweetheart. Your soul mate is here, my love."

Eddie's body heaved and stiffened on the couch. The pain in his head disappeared as Ryder entered his mind and spirit. Then he received what he would later call "the gift of the eternal now."

In an instant—or was it a century?—somewhere unchained by time, Eddie found himself one with Ryder. With Lucifer, his enemy, his soul mate. He was god and devil, and he experienced ten million years of life outside of time, with no body of his own. And still alive.

As a mortal, Eddie could conceive of nonlinear time, but he could not actually perceive time passing in any way but linear.

As long as one remains mortal, in the path of linear time, mastered by it, he must rely on something we call memory. Memories are the shadow of mortal experience.

In Eddie's mortal linear time, the shadows faded and changed unavoidably. They altered themselves with new experiences and the new memories they created and left in their wake. And the memories, old and new, would fade and blur with time.

An immortal time traveler is not bound by linear experiences, and their memories are less like shadows. The experience is not diluted. The sum total of their experiences can be perceived all at once.

And all of this Eddie now understood for the first time.

As a mortal, with linear time as his puppet master, he had a sense of solitary self and a personal identity. He had an idea of the past that helped him decide and determine his choices and decisions in his present and helped to shape his future.

We all use those ideas of the past to try to plan and direct our futures.

The mortal version of Eddie romanticized the past and strained to glimpse the future through rose-colored spectacles.

Many mortals do this with such vigor and passion that their present often finds them idle and ignorant.

"What do you want to be when you grow up?" asked the child Eddie's father, his teachers, babysitters, neighbors, friends, relatives, and role models.

His counselors and advisers tried to guide him toward the proper education and training to help him reach his personal goals and to fulfill his dreams.

So much preparation! Seeking the experiences that will form the right memories to direct our paths into their future. Directions to find fulfillment in the future and in the future of our futures.

Will we marry? Will we procreate? Are we healthy enough to survive long into the future?

When we die, when we reach the end of our time, what will we leave behind as memory? How will others remember each of us? Will our consciousness live beyond the body's demise?

All of these questions are moot in nonlinear time and thus moot to Eddie from this moment forward.

His past could be his present. The future has already been experienced. As an immortal, he could affect his past in his future as easily as his future in his past or present.

This was not the beginning of Eddie's immortality. It could be argued that there was, in fact, no beginning or cause to his immortality. Immortality simply is.

This was, however, the moment Eddie became aware of his true nature as an immortal. It was like Ryder had brought the Jungian collective consciousness into Eddie's individual consciousness all at once.

A one-eyed human may understand the science and the method of Holusion art. He can only see the flat surface of the image, however, and the three-dimensional image does not appear to him. It was the same with the mortal version of Eddie who was trapped in linear time.

Perception of linear time and Marisian time (so named after Dr. Henry Maris) is like the difference of perceiving the flat paper surface and perceiving the three-dimensional image that seems to appear like magic on the page when looked at just right.

This so-called magic is a trick played on the eyes, Eddie surmised when first he saw a Holusion art picture in a store window. His sense of sight was fooled. But was it really fooled? Perhaps through allowing his eyes to alter their perception, his mind had understood something on a deeper level.

Just as through reading the mind turns ink on paper into something much more, turns it into something wondrous and fantastic into pure imagination.

What was the truer nature of the printed page? Was it a flat-surfaced collection of wood pulp pressed together and stained with ink, or was it a murder mystery, an office memo, an eagle soaring high over steep mountains?

Of course, both were true and just as real. It was ink on a flat page of paper. And it was a beautiful image that told him a story, touched his heart, and brought his imagination to life.

Were not even mortals both flesh and spirit although one being? Did they not exist as truly as flesh and as spirit?

What Eddie now felt was a dramatic change of perception, not unlike the first time one sees the magic three-dimensional image in a piece of Holusion art and the flat page comes alive.

It was a perception felt not only in his five senses, but also in his soul. His mind. His very being.

When Adam bit into the forbidden fruit, his perception changed on the same level. He became aware of good and evil, according to the legend.

More likely, he became aware of linear time. He became aware that he had an origin and that he would have a death. He became aware of his mortality. That time would end. That he would end.

Once, Eddie thought he could defeat linear time by procreation or by leaving a written memoir. To become a legend after death was the way to outlive one's death.

This is all, outside of religion, that any mortal can hope for. In religion, one forms ideas of the life that comes when the body has died. It is the mortal dreaming of immortality.

Eddie now knew all religions had it somewhat right, though mostly wrong. Now, he had become one with every being that ever lived on Earth. And yet his heart ached with a great sense of boredom and loneliness.

Mystery, the future, the what-is-it was all gone now. The question marks that keep mortals going, the wonder and amazement of mortality and linear time melted away in a flash.

This may seem a small price to pay for immortality, but that will-crushing stripping of all questions was the evil, Eddie now knew, in Duncan's gift. That was Lucifer's intention and bitter motivation.

*****

This is how the Almighty God believing himself to be a young male nurse named Tyler Christiansen came to meet a man he would fall instantly in love with despite that his love would never be returned by the straight boy with a broken back.

Tyler's first day of work was on the night shift on a cold December night. He parked his green Volkswagen bug, and before he reached the door of Cheney Home, his new employer, he came across a pair of white underpants dancing in the night. As he got close, he could see Elias Parker's grinning face.

"Hello, my dear!" The Prophet smiled. Tyler smiled back. He liked to be called "my dear." The man in the dancing underpants seemed like an old friend to Tyler. He had no idea why.

"What are you doing in the cold outdoors in nothing but your underpants?" Tyler asked with the kindest voice he could manage.

"A moon dance."

"But there's no moon out tonight."

"Really?"

"That's right, buddy," came a voice from the edge of the driveway.

Tyler followed the voice and saw, for the first time, his future love. A handsome young man wheeled his chair into the parking lot area where Tyler had just met the Prophet and his dancing underpants.

"It's a marvelous night for a moon dance," the handsome man sang. "But you know what, buddy?"

"What's that, my friend?"

"That song is about October skies, and this is December."

"That's true," Tyler said.

"Why don't you push me back inside where it's warm, and you can dance in there?" The man smiled up at him. Still smiling, he winked at Tyler, which made him feel a strange sense of warmth.

"Okay, my friend."

The cute boy in the wheelchair looked up at Tyler. "You must be the new night nurse," he said. "I'm Duncan Ryder. This is my roommate Elias Parker. We're on B Wing."

Elias turned the wheelchair around and began to push Ryder up the sidewalk.

"I'm Tyler Christiansen. I work on B Wing starting tonight."

"Welcome to Cheney Home." Duncan smiled warmly.

The last nurse who had tried to persuade the Prophet to come indoors met them halfway and gently put a blanket around Elias's shoulders. "Hi," she said to Tyler. "I'm Beverly. We met last Friday when you toured the facility."

"Oh yes, I remember."

"This is Elias Parker. He frequently gets out, and we have to send his roommate, Duncan here, to retrieve him. For some reason, Duncan is the only one he'll listen to."

"It is about to snow," Elias said.

"I would not doubt it," Duncan replied, as Beverly opened the door for the rest of them.

Tyler did not know why, but somehow Duncan's voice made him shiver more than the cold outdoor air. Something about the young man seemed oddly familiar and exotic at the same time. He felt a strange kind of déjà vu about their meeting.

***

"Someone get Duncan," said the Almighty God in the form of Nurse Beverly. "Mr. Parker is in the old chapel and won't come out."

Tyler went down to the TV lounge where Ryder was watching CNN, as he often did in the evenings. When he got insomnia, he sometimes watched television all night long.

"Hey, Duncan," he said, "can you come with me to the old chapel? The Prophet is refusing to come back to the wing." Even in this new reality, Tyler and Duncan had begun to call Elias Parker "the Prophet."

Ryder was uncomfortable about the chapel. Every time he visited, the hairs on the back of his neck stood up. He'd been in many a church without that creepy feeling, but he felt like there were ghosts present in the old chapel—ghosts he did not believe in, but sensed there nonetheless.

Today, as he approached the chapel with Tyler, he felt flooded with warmth and even arousal, but he could not figure out why.

The Prophet was standing at the pulpit when they got there.

"Glad you could make it." He grinned as Duncan and Tyler entered the room that Duncan had always avoided since he first came to Cheney Home a few years back. "Both of you should be here for this. This is your moment."

"Our moment? What do you mean?" Tyler asked. He too was feeling a strange arousal, but he often felt a warmth and arousal when he was with Duncan.

"It is your last night together." The Prophet smiled "For now, at least."

What the Prophet was referring to was this was the very night that Tylee had rendezvoused with Ryder before their destinies were altered and their roles reversed. In the other time line, at this moment, Tylee was speaking to Ryder. But they could not hear her words.

The Prophet said her words for them. "Say you love me," he said, confusing the couple of destiny.

"I care about you and your best interests," Duncan said. "Is that close enough for you?"

"Not me, my friend. Tell her you love her."

The nurse and patient looked at one another, perplexed. Neither knew what "her" the skinny little man was referring to.

"Her!" he repeated, pointing to Tyler. "Tell Tylee you love her."

Tyler felt a flood of warmth at the very suggestion. It was also the first time in his life he had heard of the name "Tylee." He liked it, though. It sounded right and proper.

"He loves you," the Prophet said, looking at the front pew.

Duncan followed his gaze and got the strangest feeling that the "her" the Prophet referred to was really there. She was there in the front row. His penis moved in his pants as blood poured into it. He had no idea what to say, so instead he coughed loudly.

"Come on, buddy," he stammered. "It's time to get ready for bed for the night."

"Don't you want to stay for this?" Elias said.

"No, I don't," he said honestly. "This place gives me the creeps."

"Me too," Tyler admitted. It feels haunted.

"Of course it's haunted!" The Prophet smiled, sending a simultaneous chill down the pair of spines.

"Very well," the Prophet said, stepping out from behind the pulpit. In that moment, Ryder noticed a bulge in the

Prophet's pants. He appeared as aroused as Ryder himself had become.

As easily as Duncan spied Parker's partial erection, he now became aware that his own boner must be showing. And to be sure, Tyler would have noticed the bulge under any other circumstances, but he was fighting his own erection that came when Parker told Duncan to tell "Tylee" that he loved her.

And so it was that three bulging men made their way from the old chapel back to the nurse's station on B Wing. Two of the men were trying to think about something other than sex.

Elias was not thinking about other things. He was the only one of the three still in the moment. "Sorry about you losing your job," he said to Duncan, who didn't really hear him and would not have understood if he had heard.

***

This is how the Almighty God believing himself to be Eddie Maris became the one true God.

You already know how Eddie was reborn of a virgin named Mary. And you know that after he died on the cross that first Good Friday, he rose again in three days' time.

That Good Friday was the first death of the Almighty God. At that moment of death, his soul went into the rift just as the soul of Duncan Ryder had done some two thousand years later.

That purest of souls, the soul of God, was then reborn into the body of a man named Gautama, the Buddha.

He lived the lives of Ra, Muhammad, Moses, Odin, Zeus, and Abraham. He lived the lives of countless gods, prophets, and kings. He lived the lives of poor men and beggars. He lived the lives of billions of people. He lived the life of a little black beetle until it was stomped to death by a seventh-grade child named Duncan Ryder. Men, women, children who died in the womb; animals; and trees—he lived them all before returning to that form of Christ in three days' time. He had lived and died a trillion, trillion times and more.

He lived your life, lived mine, and lived Duncan Ryder's life, lived Tylee's and Tyler's, too many lives for humans to count.

Not only did he die for all of us, but he died AS all of us, lived as all of us.

He then appeared in the otherwise lifeless body of the man called Jesus in which he walked the Earth one last time. Then he went, body and soul together, into the rift where he remains eternal.

***

This, my friend, is how the Almighty God created the heavens and the Earth. It is how the universe began.

Time, the fourth dimension, is an illusion of the physical universe. It is how we can perceive movement, change, and separateness. In the rift, linear time does not exist.

All that is in the rift is one, is in the same moment, free of time.

As we all know, time began at the big bang. The entire universe existed in one form, a singularity. You also know that in the beginning, God created the heaven and the Earth.

We also know that everything created must be created out of something. We know that matter and energy can be neither created nor destroyed.

So before time began, before the big bang, what existed out of which to create the universe? God is the answer. God existed before time, and God created the universe out of the only material that existed before time—God.

This is why we say "the Almighty God" in the form of all that is is created by God out of God. You are God. I am God. Eddie Maris is God. Duncan Ryder, the devil, is God.

The universe was thus created: Ryder, the devil, wanted to be like God, wanted to be the one true God.

Thus, he attempted to kill God where no time existed, within the Marisian Rift. When time began, God expelled Lucifer from heaven. You know this already.

The timeless rift was and is the singularity out of which God expelled Lucifer. But within the rift, the two are one, and both are one with the rift. This expulsion was the source, the big bang.

It was the beginning of time and space, the beginning of the universe as we understand it. And as I have said before, time, the fourth dimension, is an illusion. It is an illusion of mortality, of motion, of change, of separateness.

**

This is how the Almighty God in your form, believing himself to be you, will leave your body and go to another place when you die.

Every soul leaves their body behind at death and goes into the singularity that is the Marisian Rift. There they join with the spirit of God and become a small part of the whole of God. Or else they join with the spirit that is Lucifer. You know these two existences as heaven and hell.

Then part of God and part of Lucifer join and becomes a new person. This is commonly known as reincarnation. Because your spirit, or soul if you prefer, comes from the Almighty God and from hell as well; just as our body is formed by a sperm and an egg joined together, each of our souls have a duality. A potential within the very soul to be either good or evil.

This is just the same as how the body can be either male or female, but both genders have at least one X chromosome and another X or a Y.

The body comes from two; the spirit comes from two.

The mixture is not always even and balanced, and thereby some people are born with an unbalanced soul. Born without a sense of empathy, they become sociopathic, for example. They are people we may call pure evil.

This duality is true of even the human who was born as the very Son of God.

Christians believe his blood gives them everlasting life. And surely, it was the blood from his nose introduced into the pool of what has been called the primordial soup that created life on Earth, as I have already told you.

So in a very real way, it is life-giving blood.

When you have said "the devil made me do it," you spoke the truth for a portion of the devil's soul is part of what makes you you.

Now, I am the Almighty God calling himself Jonah. Before now, I was the Almighty God calling himself Eddie Maris. Now I have come to my Nineveh to share this story with you. After this, I will join with the oneness, will become God, will become you, and become everyone you have ever met or even heard of and imagined

You, the Almighty God believing himself to be you, now go and be the best you that you can be. See the God in everyone. In every living thing.

When you die, and die you will, I will be waiting to welcome you to paradise, the oneness with God. For now, I bid you goodbye and Namaste.

ABOUT THE AUTHOR

Jay P. Michaels began his writing career as a journalism major at the University of Nebraska where he wrote for the campus daily newspaper. At about that time, the newspaper business was suffering from the rise of the internet, and Jay began to focus instead on art and put the idea for this, his first novel, on the back burner. Then after a move to a warmer climate, he wrote and produced a couple of plays and co-wrote a few musicals. He then decided to leave the plays to a friend and focus his attention on this novel that had been simmering for so many years. He has paid his bills with side jobs including geriatrics and other health care career positions. Never satisfied, he moved through several jobs including as managing editor for a monthly magazine, an administrative assistant, a library worker, and even in sales. Through all those career changes, his passion for writing remained mostly dormant. Until he found success as a playwright, that is. With that wind in his sails, he again found his muse.

CPSIA information can be obtained
at www.ICGtesting.com
Printed in the USA
FSHW04n1831220318
45822FS